Other Books by Silver James

Moonstruck Genesis:

Moonstruck: Secrets
(Contains the novellas Blood Moon and Bad Moon plus additional chapters and cut scenes)
Moonstruck: Lies
(Contains the novellas Hunter's Moon and Wolf Moon plus additional chapters and cut scenes)

Moonstruck:

*Blood Moon – Book 1
*Bad Moon – Book 2
*Hunter's Moon – Book 3
*Wolf Moon – Book 4
*Bride's Moon – Book 5
*Rogue Moon – Book 6
*Christmas Moon – A Moonstruck Novella (#7)
*Blue Moon – Book 8
*Moon Shot – Book 9
(A Moonstruck/Hard Target Crossover Novel)
*Dallas Fire & Rescue: Blood & Fire
(A Moonstruck companion novella set in
Paige Tyler's Dallas Fire & Rescue Kindle World)
*Special Forces: Operation Alpha: Rescue Moon
(A Moonstruck novella set in Susan Stoker's Special
Forces: Operation Alpha Kindle World)
*Special Forces: Operation Alpha: SEAL Moon
(A Moonstruck novella set in Susan Stoker's Special
Forces: Operation Alpha Kindle World)

The Cowboy's Christmas Proposition RDR#7

From Wild Rose Press:
Faerie Fate
Faerie Fire
Faerie Fool
*Faerie Reign
(Digital 3-book boxed set at a special price)
*Faerie Faith (Twelve Brides of Christmas)

Class of '85 Reunion Series:
*Fairy Tales Can Come True
*Promises, Promises

Dearly Beloved Series:
*Best Laid Plans

*Available in digital format only

NIGHT MOVES
Nightriders MC #2

—————

Silver James

Contact: silverjames@swbell.net

Cover design © by *Clary Carey*, clarycarey@gmail.com
Images: www.depositphotos.com
Caucasian Male Face Portrait ©alonesdj
Motorcycle in flames ©3quarks
Wolf jump illustration ©I.Petrovic
Edited by Gregory Alan

First Print, United States of America 2017
ISBN-10: 0-9969994-3-4
ISBN-13: 978-0-9969994-3-4

9 8 7 6 5 4 3 2 1

DEDICATION

To my readers—old and new, who demand more from me, who make me want to tell great stories, and who make me smile with their reviews and encouragement. Y'all are the reason I do what I do.

ACKNOWLEDGEMENTS

Writing is the one profession where the voices in my head mean I'm not totally bat-shit crazy when I talk back to them. I love my voices, even when they argue with me. Which they do. Way more than they should. Silly buggers.

As always, many thanks to my readers, the Facebook crew at Silver James: For Readers, friends, and family.

I truly appreciate the help I receive from my critique partner Heidi, beta reader Siobhan, and cover artist Clary for the many "do-overs" until we get things right. I couldn't do what I do without the help and guidance of my wonderful husband aka Lawyer Guy. Last but definitely not least, I want to recognize the fans of each of my series. Each email, Facebook comment, tweet, and visit to my website convinces me that the Wolves, Nightriders, Hard Target Team, and denizens of the Penumbra Papers all deserved to see the light of day.

One last caveat: Any and all mistakes are my own.

ONE

HOLLYWOOD

NO BIMBO HAS ever slept in my bed. If she's still there at dawn, she hasn't been sleepin' and I've been up all night. That was the case now as I walked the woman through the clubhouse to the front parking lot and the Mercedes convertible the same color as her clingy red dress. Two of the brothers who'd crashed in the clubhouse offered drunken thumbs up as a third offered to take her off my hands. Her fancy bra and panties were dangling from one of her hands and that dress left nothing to a man's imagination.

I got her installed in the driver's seat, buckled up, car started and pointed in the right direction then I headed back inside. Once she was clear of Nightrider territory, she was no longer my problem. Her voice calling my name made me turn around.

"Eric! Did you keep my card, darling? I'm serious about representing you if you want to model."

Yeah, like that was going to happen in my fucking lifetime. Why the hell I'd told her my given name was beyond me at the moment. The hulking presence at my back and his mocking laughter didn't help my mood much.

"Damn, dude. Fashion model?" Gravedigger Cole, Nightrider MC enforcer and all-round asshole Wolf. Just my luck. "You ain't gonna go…"

I waited for it, rolling my eyes.

"…all Hollywood on us, are you?"

I growled and threw the first punch. Two seconds later, we were whaling on each other in a friendly free-for-all. Digger had me by almost six inches and forty pounds, but I was sneakier. I wrapped my hand around his balls. First mistake. Second was letting go. I hit the side of the building face first.

Three minutes later, Hardass Tyree, national VP and all-round medic, was cleaning me up—none too gently.

"Dumb ass. Keep this up and that face of yours won't be so pretty anymore."

I held the wadded-up gauze he handed me to my nose to help clot the blood. I was Wolf so I'd heal fast—well, faster than a human would.

Digger slid down the wall beside me and accepted the cold pack Hardy held out to him. "You still hit like a girl, Hollywood."

My gaze flicked to the bruise spreading on his jaw. "Yeah, and you squeal like a teenager at a Bieber concert."

Hardy choked back a laugh. "Now that's just mean, Wood."

"Hey, gotta get my licks in where I can."

"Well, take your licks and get on your bike, since you're awake. The Russian got word that Hell Dogs have been sighted out toward Topeka. Deadhead asked for some recon help." Hardy glanced at Digger. "You go with him."

Deadhead was president of the Nightriders' Topeka chapter. The fuckin' Hell Dogs, a rival MC, had been quiet the last few months. Before they went underground, they kidnapped two of our women—brutalized them and threatened the kids belonging to Easy Cross, another enforcer. Nightriders don't take that shit. The Russian, our national prez, sent out the call. When we rolled, there was a blood bath. Since then, the fuckin' Dogs nibbled around our edges but never stuck around long enough to get caught. Our national HQ was in Mission Springs, Missouri, just outside Kansas City, and Topeka was too damn close for comfort.

Digger stood up, reached down and grabbed my hand, hauling me to my feet. "C'mon. I'll buy you breakfast at Momma's."

My stomach rumbled. Yeah. A huge stack of Momma's buttermilk pancakes, a pound of bacon and sausage and a gallon of coffee would fix me right up.

Thirty minutes later, we rolled up in front of Momma's Kitchen. The place was open 24/7 and served breakfast anytime. Momma was a big black guy who'd spent 30 years in the Marine Corps serving up food in the worst corners of the world. He'd taken his retirement pay, bought a couple of derelict train cars and built this diner. Nothing fancy about the place or the food but every bite was damn tasty.

The bleary-eyed waitress poured our coffee, took our order, and shuffled off for a cigarette break. Momma got pissy when Alice smoked around the food though I remember one night when Mom was gone four of us made bets on how long the ash on the cig jammed in the corner of Alice's mouth would stay on. Damn if that bitch lasted more than an inch before it ashed out into Digger's coffee cup. Digger didn't leave a tip but the rest of us did. It was awesome.

We didn't talk while waiting for our food. There was nothing to say. We were brothers. We drank, we fought for and against each other, we fucked, though I wasn't really one to share. Life was good. Except for the Hell Dogs. And some shit about scary black ops types wanting our DNA.

Not every Nightrider is a Wolf. The majority of us are, but it seemed like all the new prospects were Wolves. And there are Wolves all over—outlaws and white hats both. Technically, we're *lupi versi pellis*. Literally translated, it means the man who wears the skin of a wolf. We're wolf shifters, not skinwalkers. There's an animal half we carry inside us, almost like a separate entity but we're joined at the soul with our animal. Any time we want a good laugh, we get a keg and do a werewolf movie marathon. The joke's on

Hollywood—no pun intended.

The door slammed open and two cops walked in. Great. Could my day get any better? I'd known the big one for years. He sauntered over like he owned the place.

"Well, as I live and breathe if it isn't little Eric Hilton."

Huh. Original. I offered him the smile I save for the bar flies hoping to ride me home. The hair on the back of my neck prickled as Digger sat up and took notice. His snarled message was sub-vocal but Wolves have wolf hearing, even in human form.

"He keeps hassling Nightriders, he won't be living and breathing long."

I snorted out a laugh, coffee spewing. "This is a little outside your beat, Officer Gerald."

"Didn't expect to see you scumbags out in the light of day."

I made big, I'm-scared eyes and said, "Ooooh." Gerald didn't look impressed so I added, "You want something or are you polluting our air just for the fun of it?"

Gerald lunged for me but his partner grabbed his arm and hauled him back with an urgent, "Not here. Too many witnesses."

Huh. So the pansy-ass cop had another serious hard-on for me. I wondered what I'd done to chap his ass this time. Alice arrived with breakfast and a gimlet eye for the cops.

"We don't give discounts," she drawled. "You want food or coffee, sit your butts down. You just here to hassle my customers, there's the door. Don't let it hit you in the ass on the way out."

Damn. Who knew the old broad had that much fire? Gerald's partner yanked him toward the door muttering about how they couldn't afford any more disciplinary actions. Yeah, I needed to look into those fuckers. Digger caught my eye and nodded. We'd find out what that shit was all about sooner or later. First though, Mom's most excellent pancakes, a half dozen eggs over easy, a pile of bacon, and another cup of hot coffee. I'd hunt cop another day. Next on the agenda was hunting Hell Dogs.

TWO

LAINEY

I HITCHED MY messenger bag higher on my shoulder and stared at the front entrance. The building, located in an industrial area on the highway from Mission Springs to Kansas City, didn't look like much this time of day. Under the hesitant morning sun, the place looked tired and tawdry. Honestly, it hadn't looked like much the one time I'd driven past it at night. The parking lot had been filled with guy toys—big trucks, motorcycles, hot cars, and bright lights gave the illusion of glamour.

Glancing at the big sign wrapped in dead neon, I swallowed the bile threatening to burn my throat. Chasin' Tail. Gentlemen's Club. Only no gentleman would be caught dead here. It was a strip joint plain and simple. The paper taped to the front door mocked me.

DANCERS WANTED
OPEN TRY-OUTS TODAY ONLY

I squared my shoulders. I had no choice. Snagging the brass handle, I managed to drag the heavy door open and slip inside before it closed. Squinting, I waited for my eyes to adjust from bright sunlight to inky club interior. A bunch of aromas assailed my nose— stale beer, body odor, smoke, both acrid from tobacco and sweet from marijuana. I couldn't do this. I turned to run but the door opened behind me and a tall man walked in.

He perused me in an assessing way then grinned. "Auditions are that way, babe."

Crud. Forget rocks and hard spots or any other stupid figures of speech. "Yes, about that. I've changed my mind."

His eyes roamed over me again and some trick of the light made them glint. "That's too bad. A hot little bod like yours? I'm betting you could rake in three or four hundred a night."

Stunned, I stared at him from behind rapidly blinking eyelids I'd suddenly lost control of. "Three hundred?" My voice squeaked. "Dollars?"

He laughed, and I was startled by the warmth and humor in it. "Yeah, babe."

"Well..." My brain whipped through the numbers. "Okay then." I still had to inhale a few times to steady my nerves, but I pivoted and headed deeper into the club.

A man built like a heavy-weight boxer cloned from a WWE wrestler stood with his back to the door, his attention on the stage. Four girls were up there shaking their stuff. One looked like she might be sixteen, two were in their twenties and the last one was probably close to forty. The older lady wore a G-string and pasties and holy freaking goodness, I swear she had those tassels going in two different directions.

A sharp whistle from the big guy and everyone stopped. "You!" He jabbed a thick finger at the youngest. "Your fake ID didn't cut it. Out."

The girl pouted and looked like she might consider a bribe using her mouth on a certain part of his anatomy, but he snapped his fingers and two guys sprang up on the stage to usher her backstage and presumably the rear exit. Both men wore black leather vests with the same patch on the back.

The big guy turned his attention to the woman. "Babe, we both know you're too old for this shit, no matter how much talent you got."

Her face fell but she didn't say anything. Turning, she walked to a chair with a shirt draped over it. She shrugged into it. "Had to give it try. Thanks, doll."

"Tell ya what, you teach what you know to those two and whoever else I hire and I'll pay ya a hundred an hour for the lessons."

I could see her eyes glisten for a moment then she dashed the back of one hand across them. Her smile was tremulous, but her voice solid when she said, "I can do that."

The two remaining women stared at each other then the guy standing below the stage.

"Does that mean we're hired?" one asked.

"Yeah. You're provisional. You learn from

Cookie, I'll hire you on full time."

They squealed and hugged each other. The men in the room winced and I was reminded of the one time my mother forced me to enter a beauty pageant. I still had nightmares.

"Yo, Hoss. We got one more."

I'd all but forgotten the man standing beside me. He nudged me forward and walked me right up to the big man. Just like my escort, this Hoss person looked me up and down.

"You ever dance before?"

I stared at him. Was he the owner? Or maybe he was the manager. He was tall, wide, also wore a leather vest, and hadn't shaved in several days. He scared the heck out of me but hey, nothing ventured, nothing gained, right?

"Um…not like this. Exactly." And I wouldn't be dancing like this at all if my need for money wasn't so desperate.

"Like this. Exactly. You mean you've never danced naked?

"Wait…naked? I thought the dancers wore G-strings and…uh…bras."

"We'll discuss that. Are you a dancer or not?"

"Only recreationally. But I was a gymnast."

"What's that mean? Exactly."

"I'm flexible." I eyed the stage behind the man. "Watch." Brushing past him, I placed my hands on the edge and hopped up, like I was getting out of a pool. Planting my butt on the lip of the stage, I sat for a second, getting my nerve up. My fingers brushed over the wooden surface, finding each knick and crack. Unable to stall any longer, I swung my legs around, and stood. Approaching the metal pole like it might bite me, I screwed up my mouth and considered options. I shrugged and tossed a sheepish smile at the guy. "Okay, this might be a little easier with some music."

"Yo, Wiz, hit the soundtrack." The big guy bellowed like there was a crowd in the room.

Music belched from a dozen speakers and I clapped my hands over my ears. "Can you turn it down?" I shouted over the noise. Moments later, I could actually hear the music, catch the beat. It was something slow, sensual, with a driving bass that reverberated in my chest. Not what I expected—or was used to—but yeah, I could work with this.

I let my hips loosen and move on their own while I kicked off my cowboy boots. I made a mental note to dig out a rosin powder bag if I got the job. Wiping my hands on my jeans, I hopped, raising one knee high and then charged three steps into a front walk-over. My landing put me next to the pole.

I walked around it—slowly. *Slinky. I need to think slinky. With a side of sexy.* After another hop, I grabbed the pole several feet above my outstretched hands, rolled my hips and legs until I was upside down, one knee hooked around the pole to anchor me. Too bad they didn't have aerial silk rigged. Maybe if I got the gig I could talk them into it. Doing an act like that, I wouldn't have to be naked because I could hide in the cloth.

Using the pole to my advantage, I arched and slithered, twirled and snaked up and down the apparatus. When the song ended, I curved around the pole to land on my hands and did a back walk-over to stand upright.

"Like I said, I used to be a gymnast. This isn't exactly the balance beam, but I can work the pole." I glanced down at the manager. Well fudgecicles. He had a woody the size of Cincinnati. "Uhm…I guess you liked it?"

"Damn, babe. You do that naked and you'll be rollin' in twenties if not hundreds."

"I sure hope so." Dang it. That came out sounding far more breathless and needy than it should have.

"Can you start tonight? One of our regulars called in sick."

"Oh…I…uhm…sure. I think I can get a costume and stuff. What time?"

"We'll fill out the paperwork now—"

"Paperwork?" I cut him off. "What kind of paperwork?"

"The business kind. We need name, address, phone number, social security number—all that crap. You make an hourly wage. That's paid by check and we take out all the applicable taxes. The tips? Those are all yours to do with as you please, though you'd be smart to give a cut to the bartenders and waitresses, especially if you do private."

"Private?" Yikes. Why did my voice pick now to squeak? "As in…like…alone with some guy in a room?"

"D'uh, babe. Yeah. The real money gets made doin' lap dances in the suites. You get them to buy one of the packages, you and the waitress make out like bandits."

"Uh...make out isn't a euphemism for anything is it?"

"We don't whore our girls. A dancer wants to do that on her own? That's her business and it's done off property. We run a legitimate business here."

Legitimate? Yeah, right, but if I made the kind of money they were talking about without having do anything but dance, they could be mass murderers for all I cared. "Awesome blossom. Let's do this. I need to go home and make a costume."

THREE

HOLLYWOOD

DIGGER AND I met up with Deadhead and a couple of his boys at a truck stop outside of Topeka. There were three unknown bikes parked at the motel next door. When we discovered the desk clerk was female, the brothers decided I should saunter on over there to question her. I wasn't sure I appreciated the rep but whatever. I like women. Women liked me. They went away satisfied. I left with a happy dick. Win-win, right?

When the front entrance doors slithered open, the clerk looked up with a bright smile on her face, until she saw me. She backed away from the desk, her eyes wide and frightened. I held up my right hand, palm toward her in that universal sign of "I won't hurt you."

"Easy, babe. Take a breath." I thought she might actually pass out. "I'm just here for some information. That's all." I stayed back from the counter trying to look all shucks and grins. Totally harmless. Easy should have been the one sent on this ride because he wore that look naturally.

After a few breaths, she nodded at me, straining to put a professional face on. "How may I help you, sir?"

I offered one of my charming grins. "I'm Hollywood. The bikes outside, who do they belong to?"

She blanched and her hands shook. Motherfuckers. This was a girl just trying to make a living, but she was scared shitless.

"Were they wearing cuts?"

Her brows scrunched a little and I caught a slight shake of her head, as if the question confused her. I pointed to my vest. "A cut. Colors. Either a vest or jacket with patches."

Her mouth formed an "O" and for once I wasn't thinking about how sweet it would feel around my dick. The girl was too scared and that just pissed me off.

"Y-yes."

I half-turned so she could see the leaping wolf with the comet tail that was the Nightrider patch. "Does their patch look like this?" She shook her head and took a relieved breath. "Ugly-ass dog with horns?" She pressed her lips together and nodded. "They been hassling you?" Wide-eyed, she nodded again. "Okay, darlin', you don't have worry anymore."

I stepped outside to the portico and whistled. The other Nightriders jogged over, leaving their bikes mostly out of sight at the truck stop. They came in the door behind me.

"Topeka is Nightrider territory. These assholes are trespassing. We'll take care of it." I pointed to Deadhead, watching the clerk closely. "This is the prez of the local chapter. You have any more problems with bikers, whether they're wearin' Hell Dog cuts or some other patch, you let him know. Understood?"

She hadn't blinked yet, but slowly nodded. "Okay." Her voice was a scared whisper.

"Don't get me wrong, babe. We're outlaws, but we don't hassle civilians for the fun of it. Yeah?"

The clerk nodded again. "Yeah." Her voice was a little stronger.

"Now what rooms are they in?"

Glancing over her shoulder into the office behind her, she squared her shoulders. "I shouldn't do this but..." She glanced at us. "One-thirty-two, four, and six." She moved to the counter, grabbed three plastic cards. "Hang on a sec." After doing something with the card keys and a machine, she set them on the counter. "Please don't break the doors. My manager will get upset and I can't afford to lose this job. Those are masters."

Deadhead growled under his breath. "Your job is safe, honey." He grabbed one of the motel's business cards and a pen, jotted down a number and pushed it across the counter to her. "You have any trouble, call. That phone is always answered."

I scooped up the keys, nodded to her. "The club owes you."

"Yes." Gravedigger agreed. Yeah, I'd sort of made promises not mine to make, but Digger had a soft spot for soft women. And he was part of the cadre. His agreement cemented my vow. This girl would be watched and kept safe.

Deadhead, Digger, and I each took a key and prowled across the lobby area. The three other Nightriders headed outside to station themselves by the bikes. When we flushed the Hell Dogs, they'd either stand and fight—thus dying, or they'd run, going through the windows and our brothers would take them down in the parking lot.

I paused at the first door. Sniffed. Listened. Nothing. The room was empty. I moved to join Deadhead at his door. Same thing. Empty. We converged on the third door. Digger smiled but instead of glee showing in his eyes, there was only the red flicker of a feral Wolf.

The stench of our prey filled our noses. Human, all three of them. Muted voices rumbled behind the door and we listened for a few minutes. Interesting. They were hoping to catch a solitary Nightrider to "teach the bastards a lesson." I wondered if they were here under orders or free-lancing—not that it mattered. They were in our territory and the clubs were at war.

Deadhead used his key and was the first through the door. We caught the Hell Dogs by surprise. They all went for weapons but not one got off a shot. We subdued them— handcuffs and bandanna gags—and waited for

Deadhead's riders to join us. We didn't want to make trouble for the clerk or the motel. Blood is hell to get out of carpet, not to mention the cops get involved. This was club business. No cops.

We waited to take them outside until a nondescript white van was backed up to the rear entrance, doors open. The Topeka brothers hustled the Dogs inside and the van took off. We'd question them at the Topeka clubhouse.

Digger went through the rooms, stuffing everything into a duffel bag. More riders arrived and took off with the Dogs' bikes. Digger left with Deadhead while I returned the keys and informed the clerk her guests had checked out.

She was still big-eyed and nervous so I handled her with care. "You have Deadhead's number. Use it if you need help, yeah?"

Looking uncertain, her chin jerked down in a short affirmation. I winked and grinned. "We're only scary to the bad guys." I leaned closer, looking around conspiratorially. "And don't tell anyone, but Deadhead's wife and kids think he's a big ol' teddy bear."

That got a tentative smile and a quick look down before she returned my gaze with a bit more confidence so I added, "Hopefully, you won't ever need to call, but you're a friend of the Nightriders now. We take care of our own."

Her smile grew before her expression sobered. "Will those rooms need—"

"No," I cut her off. "Two of the rooms were empty. The third one will need usual maid turn around. We're cool."

My phone beeped and I turned to read the text and leave.

"Thank you," she called after me. I tossed a half-wave in reply as I trotted to my bike. Time to get to work. We had Hell Dogs to question.

FOUR

LAINEY

GAZING AT THE full-length mirror in the dancers' dressing room, I was pretty darn impressed with my seamstress skills. I'd found a tiny bikini in a peach color that almost matched my skin tone. Using a couple of yards of fringe, a borrowed sewing machine, and a hot-glue gun, I'd made my first costume. The fringe covered up the fact I wasn't nude underneath. It left a lot to the audience's imagination but still provided a place to put money.

Whew. My modesty would be maintained but I could look sexy enough to elicit tips. Win-win. That was my new motto. Mantra. Battle cry. Win-win. I'd get on that stage tonight and start making enough money to get out of this mess. Win. Once I was out of this mess, I could keep dancing to pay for school. Win. With my degree, I could get a real job and pass my certification to become a CPA. Win. See?

This was my mindset as I plopped down in front of a cracked mirror to fluff out my hair and apply another coat of mascara to my eyelashes. The other dancers all wore falsies—eyelashes, not boobs. Nope, their "girls" were all hanging out there front and center. The crack in the glass bisected my face, and considering my current mindset, I had no hope of not waxing philosophical.

Six months ago, my life had been...okay, not wonderful precisely, but on track. My life had never been wonderful, but I was trying my best to get out of the muck and on the road to something normal. Of course, in my world, normal was a relative term. It's a cliché, but true—if you looked up *dysfunctional family* in a psychology textbook, you'd find my family portrait. Neglectful mom, absent father, lazy older brother, me, and the twin terrors who were my little brothers.

I worked through high school, worked after graduation, saved up money, and I was finally able to fund my first year of college. No scholarships, no Pell Grants, no FAFSA student loans for me—not until I could shed the stigma of my family. Just me doing a series of low-paying menial jobs. But I put away enough for my tuition and books, and I continued working so I'd have enough for my second year. And then, just like the mirror I stared into, my life cracked in two.

Broken dreams. Broken life. But I refused to let misfortune break me. I wasn't some little "poor, pitiful me" looking for someone to save me. Nope. Not my style.

"Hey, Lainey."

Cookie's hail pulled me out of the rabbit hole. She stood in the door with a wad of bright blue silk in her hand. "Hoss says he needs to talk to you. Out at the bar."

She tossed the cloth at me and I grabbed it. Shaking it out, I discovered a short—as in barely-covered-my-butt short—kimono-style robe.

"Put that on and get your sweet ass out there. There's a few customers comin' in. You don't want to give it away for free."

"Oh, um, thanks." I slipped my arms through the sleeves and belted it. The robe covered more than I'd anticipated.

The sound system was pumping out rock and roll but not at a level that would deafen me. I glanced around but didn't see Hoss anywhere. The guy who'd followed me in that morning was behind the bar. I scurried to the end of the bar closest to the hallway leading to the dressing room and hopped up on a stool. The guy acknowledged me but continued filling a mug with beer from a tap. He set it down on the bar in front of a heavy-set guy with grease smeared across his cheekbone. At least I hoped it was grease and not a bruise.

The bartender visited with his customer for a couple of minutes while I looked around. I hadn't paid much attention my first trip through the doors. The place was about the size of a large high school gymnasium. Tables of various heights with chairs and stools filled the space. Maybe twenty-five guys occupied the place, singly or in groups. The bar stretched along one wall. The stage was narrow but long, with two poles, one at each end. There was also an intersecting stage that ran perpendicular and it, too, had a pole near the end jutting furthest into the audience. The stage was lined with bar stools.

"Somethin' to drink, sweetcheeks?"

I swiveled around to face the bartender. He was far too good-looking for my peace of mind. "Oh, uh, sure. Water? And Cookie told me Hoss needed to speak with me?"

He scooped up ice in a glass and used the bar gun to squirt water into it. "Have you picked out your music?"

I stared at him. From his cocky grin I figured I looked totally befuddled. "Music?" I was supposed to pick out a playlist?

He laughed and tapped his finger on the end of my nose like I was a little kid...or an untrained puppy. "You're cute. Yes, music. Girls on the poles get to pick their own. The regular dancers just dance to what's on the track."

Huh. Who knew? "Oh."

The guy laughed again. "You're way out of your comfort zone, babe. You should figure out a stage name while you're picking music. And speaking of names, I'm Wizard. I also work the music machine."

Wizard? What kind of name was that? Curious, I asked.

"It's my road name."

"Road name?"

"I'm a Nightrider, babe. We're a motorcycle club. It's tradition to have road names. When we patch in as full members, we forget we have other names."

"Ah. I see, said the clueless new girl."

"So, music? And I have to say, you're pretty fuckin' hot on that pole."

I blushed and from the heat radiating from beneath the robe, it was a full body flush. Yippee. "Uh, thanks. I think."

"S'all good, babe, though I gotta say, you aren't the type we normally get in here."

"Yes, well. About that. I need to make some money. A lot of money. Quickly."

His thick brows scrunched toward the bridge of his nose and he studied me. "You in trouble?"

Uh oh. I probably should have made up something—like I was studying strippers for a research paper for a sociology class or something. I never was much good at thinking fast on my feet. I was slow and methodical, the type to like numbers and accounting. "No. Not me. It's a...family thing."

He continued to give me a narrow-eyed look but didn't pursue the topic. I felt like I'd dodged a bullet. "So...music? I admit I haven't thought much about it. I tend to listen mostly to country music. The song I danced to this morning was good. Do you have more songs like it?"

Wiz chuckled and shook his head as he

ripped the top off a beer with his hand—his *bare* hand. After a long guzzle, he said, "Most dancers rehearse. Choreograph their routines. Are you tellin' me you just climbed that pole and did what you did?"

"Pretty much, yes."

"Damn, babe, you're killin' me. I'll pick out a few songs."

"Few songs?" I blinked a couple of times, wrapping my brain around that. "I'll be dancing more than once?"

"Yeah, babe. Didn't Hoss explain? You're on once an hour between seven p.m. and two a.m. Last call is two, but the girls keep dancing until we kick the assholes out at three." He was flicking through some CDs and got a wicked grin. "You familiar with Dylan?"

I was counting up the hours up on my fingers, but glanced up. "As in Bob?"

Wizard nodded. "Yeah. Got your name right here. Lady Lay." He eyed me again. "And wear your cowboy boots. They'll go with the fringe."

I clamped my mouth shut. The name was as good as any and my boots were infinitely better than those stilts the other dancers wore. At the moment, my brain needed numbers. Math. Yes, math was good. I started counting again. Eight, nine, ten, eleven, twelve, one... Six. I had to get on that pole six times a night? I yelped softly. Good thing I'd found my rosin bag but my muscles were already screaming. I swiveled around to study the stage. I needed to work on my strutting…maybe working between the poles with shortened routines on the poles themselves, give myself a breather in between the pole work.

The lights came down and I realized Wizard wasn't standing there any longer. He and a woman were working up and down the bar. Since we'd been talking, men—and a few women—had begun to fill up the place. I was about to head backstage when a man walked through the arch between the foyer and the club itself.

My ears buzzed. My mouth went dry. I didn't breathe for a minute. He was…something. Tall, lean, dark hair, and, given his coloring, probably dark eyes—I couldn't tell at that distance under the lowered lights. He was gorgeous. And wearing a vest— which I was slowly coming to associate with motorcycle clubs in general, and the Nightriders in particular.

He might be an instant orgasm in black leather, but he was trouble. Big trouble. The kind of trouble that should have danger music for the soundtrack. He was too much of everything, especially for a girl like me. Nope. I had enough trouble, thank you very much. I certainly didn't need more, especially his brand of it. His head turned as he surveyed the room. His gaze hadn't hit the bar yet and I figured I needed to make my escape. Pronto. I ducked through the curtains sectioning off the bar from the hallway. Lady Lay needed to stop hyperventilating before she went on stage.

FIVE

HOLLYWOOD

I WALKED THROUGH the door and was checking out the crowd when a flash of blue teased the corner of my vision. I saw big hair and a sweet ass ducking behind the curtain separating the bar from the backstage. One of the dancers must have been working the bar for private dances.

Gravedigger stepped up beside me and nodded toward the bar. Wiz was waving toward two stools he'd just emptied for us. The two guys he chased off looked disgruntled until they caught sight of Digger'n me. Yeah, they were more than happy to give up their seats.

Wiz tossed a plastic bag full of ice at Digger and he wrapped it around his knuckles. The cuts and bruises would be mostly gone by morning but ice never hurt. Digger had done all the heavy hitting with the Hell Dogs. I'd just asked the questions. We'd stopped by the clubhouse and made a report to the Russian and Hardy before heading over here for booze, bar food, and some babes. Rumor had it, Hoss had some new blood in the house.

I killed my beer in a series of long swallows with the second bottle waiting when I put the first down. Digger nursed a double whiskey, one eye on the door, the other on the stage. Two women stepped into twin spotlights and the music cranked up. I had no idea how Wiz could work here night after night with all the noise. I'd been there less than ten minutes and a headache was already banging against my skull.

One of the girls was a regular, the other new. I watched for a bit then went back to drinking. The beer wouldn't numb the pain— nor would I get drunk, but it was cold and tasted good. Lolo, the female bartender working with Wiz, slid two baskets in front of us. Big, rare burgers and greasy fries. Bar food at its best.

Digger dug in and three burgers apiece later, both of us were feeling more like ourselves. Wolves have fast metabolisms. We went through food, booze, and broads in a hurry. I shifted on my stool, thinking about that glimpse of blue I'd caught. I liked long hair. There was just something about fisting it while I slammed into a woman doggie style. Damn. My dick was hard just thinking about it. I'd watch the end of this set then head back to the clubhouse. There'd be a sweet butt or three hanging around who'd take care of that hard-on for me.

I was about to call it a night when the place went dark and Wiz's voice ghosted over the loud speaker, the opening notes of Dylan's "Lay, Lady Lay" whispering just beneath his introduction.

"Chasin' Tail is pleased to announce the debut of our very own, Lady Lay…"

The music changed to something dark and driving with lots of bass and back beat. The spotlight flared to life highlighting a woman standing, legs apart, head down, hands behind her back. She wore nothing but fringe—long fringe that danced with each deep breath she took—and cowboy boots.

Tossing her head up, all that big, blonde hair flying, she bent backwards—impossibly, or so I thought until her hands touched the stage and her legs followed the rest of her body. My dick was wide awake now and I, along with every man in the joint, was staring. She strutted—no, that wasn't a strut, she oozed—all slinky sex—over to the pole on the left side of stage. When she humped that pole—fuck that. She wasn't humping the pole, she was making love to that sucker, and I almost swallowed my tongue.

The strobe lights flashed red and white and I caught the singer crooning words that sounded like "burnin' it down." Oh fuck yeah. She was burnin' down the stage and setting my dick on fire. She strutted along the front of the stage and guys were climbing up to shove money at her. She skipped, hopped, and holy fuck, did another walk-over thing that put her on the right-hand pole.

My brain stopped processing her moves but when she hit the center pole on the stretch stage, I was there front and center. My wolf was snapping and snarling to get free. He wanted to attack the men ogling this woman, wanted to rip out their throats. *Ours*, the wolf insisted.

I was ready to climb on the stage, throw her over my shoulder, and get her the fuck away from these assholes. A hand clamped on my shoulder and I spun, hands fisted, a snarl on my face. Digger, his expression grim.

He mouthed, "Club business."

Fuck. I forced my wolf down deep and followed Digger out. He didn't have to push through the crowd. One look at him, people got the hell out of the way. Out in the parking lot, we mounted our bikes and I leashed my wolf while Digger explained.

"Those Hell Dogs?"

"What about 'em?"

"One got away."

LAINEY

THE DRESSING ROOM was empty. Finally. Some of the girls were dancing, the rest were either working the floor to book private dances or taking a break out back. I could hear music from the club, muted though it was. I stared at the pile—and I mean *pile*—of money sitting on the dressing table in front of me. My hands shook as I counted it. A few ones—in their own measly stack. Fives, the same. Tens. Twenties—hundreds of dollars in twenties. And oh my god hundreds. Eleven of them.

I recounted the stacks. One thousand, nine hundred and sixty-eight dollars. I couldn't breathe. Then I started hyperventilating. I scooped all the money into my makeup bag before I put my head between my knees so I didn't faint. My night wasn't even finished yet. I had one more set to dance.

For the first time in days, I could take a deep breath that didn't hurt my chest. Maybe the light at the end of the tunnel wasn't a train after all. If I could keep this up—and I now understood why Wizard mentioned the dancers working on routines, I'd have the money I needed and I could get my life back to normal. Well, normal for me.

Cookie stuck her head in the door and looked around. "You alone, doll?" I nodded. "You should be out on the floor, hustlin'."

Anger surged and I started to explain that I was *not* a prostitute when she held up a hand. "Hustlin' for private dances, doll baby. I know you think you made a pile tonight but the big money—the easy money is doin' privates. You should be workin' the floor. The way you move? The boys'll be all over you and lookin' to pay premium for the chance to get you alone."

"Look, Cookie—"

"Hush, girl. You don't turn tricks. You ain't

that kinda gal. I got that. 'Sides, Hoss tosses out a girl for doin' that in this place. They run it clean." She laughed, a donkey's bray sort of sound. "Don't that beat all? Outlaw motorcycle club playin' legit in a sex club. What's the world comin' to?"

"Money laundering," I muttered under my breath.

One of the other dancers bounced through the door. Her candy-red hair danced in crazy curls and she hadn't belted her robe, leaving her "girls" out there front and center. "I have just enough time for a cigarette break before hitting the back room." She smiled at me. "I'm Mary Jane but Wiz always introduces me as Girly Temple." She flicked fingers through her curls. "I always get the guys who have a thing for school girls. You're Lady Lay, right?"

I blushed, unable to stop the heat flooding my cheeks. "Lainey," I introduced myself.

"Nice t'meetcha." She dug through a huge satchel bag at her dressing table, snagged a pack of cigarettes and a lighter. "Later, tater."

Mary Jane skipped out, looking young and carefree like her character. Cookie flashed me a careful smile. "That girl ain't as innocent as she looks or sounds, doll baby. You keep that in mind, yeah?"

"Oh. Yes, I will. Thanks, Cookie."

I was in the dressing room of a strip joint owned by an outlaw motorcycle club. No one who worked here was as innocent as they looked or sounded. Not even me.

SIX

HOLLYWOOD

DIGGER, EASY, AND I had been on the road for a week. Our first order of business had been to deliver the heads of two Hell Dogs to their clubhouse down in Little Rock. Well, second order. The first had been to search for the one that got away. He'd put a Nightrider in the hospital doin' it.

We'd questioned all three Dogs, got all the information they had the first day we caught them. Deadhead had them locked up in the basement of the Topeka clubhouse in case we needed trade bait. After the escape, the two still in custody were nothin' more than sacrificial assholes. When we didn't find the escapee, we made the run to Arkansas to make our point. We had to wait until dark to sneak up to the compound. Easy shifted and in wolf form, pissed on the front gates. While their idiot guards were chasing him, Digger and I stuck the heads on the spikes at the front entrance.

Then we stopped for burgers and beer.

Now we were back in Mission Springs. The

Russian was...well, hell. There wasn't a description for how pissed he was. Deadhead wasn't any better. We'd exhausted all our leads. Until we got a new one, I wanted a hot shower and a cold beer. And just maybe, a trip to Chasin' Tail. There was a dancer I wanted to get to know better. A hellava lot better.

I didn't bother going home, heading to the Barracks instead. I bypassed the clubhouse. It might be afternoon, but it was Saturday. That meant the sweet butts were struttin' their stuff in front of the brothers. As horny as I was, I should have dropped my ass right there to see what was available. Still... What had Wiz called her? Lady Lay? Oh, yeah. I was gonna lay that lady down across my bed.

My bike was parked in the yard between the clubhouse and the Barracks. The clubhouse had rooms any brother could use if he wanted a little privacy. The Barracks was just that—private rooms belonging to an individual brother. I kept a room there and it had its own bathroom. Hot shower, clean clothes, Chasin' Tail. Yeah, sounded like a plan to me. I grabbed my saddlebag from the Harley and headed inside.

While I was in the shower, hot water sluicing across muscles that'd been tense for too many days, I finally relaxed. Until I remembered Lady Lay and pictured her dancing in my head. Fuckin' A but she had a hot bod and knew how to use it. My wolf got all snarly thinkin' about other men watching her, touching her. My dick got harder when *I* thought about touching her.

With a soap-slicked palm, I fisted my hard-on and pumped. I imagined her cupping my balls and they drew up, tight, ready. Then I pictured her lips forming an "O" and sliding over the head, down the shaft. Fuck! I spewed my load. I hadn't lost control like that since I was twelve and masturbating under the sheet in my bed.

Oh yeah, I was headed to Chasin' Tail and I was gettin' me some of that.

LAINEY

I HOPPED UP on the barstool nearest the back hallway, careful to keep my robe between my butt and the seat. Not that I believed in cooties. Much. Anyway, it was mid-afternoon and things were slow and laid back. I really wanted something to drink before I hit the stage for my set. Wiz was working the bar alone. He made a couple of drinks and set them on a tray for the waitress, pulled a beer for one of the regulars, then fizzed me a Coke with the bar gun and brought it down to me. I thanked him just as Hoss, the club manager, pulled up the stool next to mine.

"Lainey."

"Hoss." The guy had something on his mind, but I'd learned in the short week I'd been here that he spoke only when he was good and ready. Wiz slid a big glass of ice water down the bar. Hoss stopped it with a cupped palm, lifted it, and drank.

"Lainey," he said again.

"Hoss." I matched his tone and delivery.

He grinned so big his eyes twinkled. "We need to talk."

Hoss looked happy—well as happy as a six-foot-four bear of an outlaw motorcycle gangster who ran a strip club could look. I wasn't worried about getting fired. My sets seemed very popular. My weekend tips had been mind-blowing. The weeknights? Not as good but still more than I made at my other two jobs combined.

Some of the other girls were muttering behind my back as a result. I was pulling in an average of a thousand a night for six to seven dances. One part of me was freaked out. The part that was totally scared about the detour my life had taken was thankful. The more money I made, the faster I could get my life back on track. I'd even quit my other part-time jobs.

"What about?"

"You dancin'."

Now I was confused and my expression reflected that.

"Private, babe. I'm gettin' lotsa requests."

"Ahhhh." I scrunched up my nose. "I'm not sure I'm ready for that."

Mary Jane slid onto the stool to my left.

"You should do it, girl. Two, three private dances a week and I've paid my mortgage *and* my car payment. 'Course, you need to split with the waitress and the bartender—give them a bigger cut than our usual ten percent when we're on stage. Still…" She gave me the once-over, her eyes trailing up, down and back up. "Considering what you rake in on the stage? Hoss is right. You could ask and get top dollar for a private."

Hoss clapped his hand on my shoulder as he heaved off the stool. "Somethin' to think about, babe. Just let me or Cookie know if you're interested."

Mary Jane finished off the OJ and vodka Wiz had fixed for her, slipped off her robe, and tossed it at me. "Take that backstage for me? I'm up next."

When her music started, she strutted across the floor, used a guy's thigh and his table to reach stage height, and did a tabletop shimmy before stepping across a slight gap to an empty barstool and then onto the stage. Huh. I was impressed.

I had three songs before my number so I tucked Mary Jane's robe over my arm, turned back to the bar, and sipped my Coke. Wiz came down to check on me.

"I'm surprised," he hollered over the music.
"About what?"
"You."
Me? What did that mean? I offered him my perplexed expression instead of trying to

shout.

"You don't seem like the type. You have an education."

Ah, now this conversation made sense. Sort of. "College takes money." So did paying off family debts.

"What are you studying?"

I could guess what his reaction would be when I replied. I was surprised when it came. "Accounting. I want to be a CPA."

"No shit?" Wiz appeared suitably impressed.

"Absolutely. I had a four point oh."

"Had?"

"I dropped out."

"Money?"

"Yeah. And family things."

"Family can be a bitch."

Mine certainly could. I had to live at home and all too often, ended up babysitting. My little brothers could be hellions if I didn't ride herd on them. The music switched over and I slugged down the rest of my Coke. "Thanks, Wiz. Later!"

Backstage, I handed the robe to Mary Jane and she plopped onto a hard plastic chair at her dressing table. Her phone pinged and she eagerly snatched it up.

"New boyfriend?"

She beamed. "Yes. He's just the best! What about you? Do you have a boyfriend?"

"I wish, but no. I didn't have time. Three jobs don't leave room for a social life."

"Damn, sweetie. That sucks."

Yes, yes it did, but maybe now I could at least dream about going on a date. But not with that hot club member I'd glimpsed last week. No, definitely not him. Oh yes, I'd get right on *not* doing that.

SEVEN

LAINEY

I HAD A BAD feeling about this. Hoss had told
me I didn't have to do private dances, even
though the money was good and he'd urged me
to do it. It took Mary Jane talking me into
taking over one of her dances to get me to
commit. She wanted to take off early to meet
her boyfriend. She'd caught me in a moment of
weakness, waving her phone at me.

"My guy got off early and wants me to shy
out early, too."

"You're off by ten tonight, right?"

"Yeah, but he's off at nine and I have a
private booked." Her expression had turned
speculative. "Why don't you take it for me? The
guy's one of the Nightriders, Lainey. A big
tipper. And because he's a Nightrider, he won't
push the rules. Just give him a good lap dance
and it's a quick five hundred. This is a huge
favor, sweetie. I won't even ask for a cut.
Please? Pleasepleaseplease. I'll owe you big
time!" She gave me air kisses and ran out the
back door.

So, an hour later, I walked into one of the

back rooms. There was a couch, an armchair, and some other furniture pushed back into the dark corners. The lights were low, the music throbbing, and the client, a big ol' teddy bear named Lug Nut, was sitting in a straight-back chair in the middle of the room.

A few minutes later, I was straddling Lug's thick thighs doing a hip roll when somebody kicked the door open. My back was to it and I never had a chance to look before I was tossed across the room to land halfway on a couch. Fists were flying and then I was in the middle of the knife and gun club.

I figured out two things right quick—I was up shit creek and the Nightriders signed my paycheck. Besides, Lug Nut was outnumbered four to one. When a honking big Bowie knife skittered my way, I snatched it up and went hunting.

One of the attackers saw me coming and threw a punch. I ducked and sliced his arm. He jerked away, bleeding. Another guy was already down and out, put there by Lug. The other two had Lug wrapped up, one holding his arms behind him while the other was beating him. The big man jerked free and went to whaling on them both. They pinned him again, and one of them pulled out a monster-sized pistol and pointed it at Lug Nut.

You know that whole fight or flight thing? Yeah, instinct took over and my daddy would have called me stupid. I jumped on the guy holding Lug and jammed the knife into his belly. He bellowed and grabbed at me right as the gun went off.

Something hot burned my cheek. I couldn't see and then I was on the floor screaming as something crushed my right wrist. A bone snapped then hot, greasy pain rocketed into my brain. Bile surged into my mouth and I choked on it.

"No. No! She saved me. Let 'er go. Don't hurt her."

There was shouting. Moaning. I think that last was me. My arm hurt. My face hurt. Some son of a buck was kneeling on my back and I couldn't breathe. Stars sparkled in the dark surrounding me. Voices echoed around me, but I only recognized one. Lug Nut. Still telling them I'd saved his life.

The pressure eased and somebody flipped me over.

"Fuck. She's been shot."

I had? Huh.

"What the hell happened to her arm?"

"She had a knife."

"So you broke her arm?"

My cheek was on fire. I reached with my left hand—my right wouldn't work—to check but somebody grabbed my hand.

"No, babe. Don't be touching."

Everything got real quiet and it felt like all the air got sucked out of the room.

"How did Hell Dogs get into the club?"

Oh. Lord. I knew that voice, that accent. The Russian, Nightrider national president and all round baddest of the bad guys. He'd been in the club a few times and everyone walked on egg shells around him.

"No cuts, Russkie. Wearin' civilian clothes."

"Lug Nut?"

"They kicked the door in, boss. Jumped me. That fucker there had me pinned 'til Lainey stuck him." He hacked up a noogie and spat. "I kicked that motherfucker right before he pulled the trigger. Missed me, hit her."

Somebody knelt beside me, helped me sit up, and I swear I heard a dog growl. A big dog.

"Wood, back off. I need to check her. Hey, sugar, I'm Hardy. I need to look at your face and your arm, yeah?"

I nodded—or thought I did—and blinked to get the sparkles to go away so I could see clearly. Not that it worked.

The guy kneeling in front of me was cute—in a really intense way. He was scruffy, hair and beard, but he had kind eyes. He dabbed at my cheek with a gauze pad.

"Ow?"

He smiled and I caught a hint of dimple. I couldn't help but smile back. Then that darn dog growled again. What was up with that? Who brings a dog to a strip joint?

Hardy glanced up at something behind me. "Bullet graze. If she's lucky, it won't scar."

Scar? On my face? Great. That would cut my tips to nothing because who wants to stick twenties in the g-string of some bimbo with a scarred face? Bummer. I suddenly felt really tired which meant all that adrenaline was about to send me into a crash.

The man with kind eyes—um, Hardy—caught my gaze and held it. "Need t'check your arm, sugar. Gonna hurt."

Yeah. With the adrenaline draining I could feel the throb running all the way up to my shoulder. I sucked in air and nodded. He picked up my hand. Oh. My. Freaking. God! *Gonna hurt* didn't even come close. I didn't mean to scream but I couldn't help it.

Arms circled my waist and muscular legs framed my naked thighs. Worn denim brushed my skin, comfortable and comforting. Something warm and hard snuggled my bare back. Smooth. Sliding against me like butter. Only with lumps. Leather. A leather vest. With buttons and patches.

"Breathe, baby. You gotta breathe." The voice, husky and gruff, rumbled in my ear.

I should have been scared and totally freaked out, but I wasn't. For the first time since I could remember, especially since those scary guys came to my mom's house, and I'd come to work at Chasin' Tail, I felt safe.

Without warning, I was picked up and shifted so that I sat in a chair, but still surrounded by warmth and hard muscles. Hardy held my arm while I was moved and it only hurt a bunch but not as bad as if my hand had been flopping around.

My vision cleared a little more and I saw Hardy look toward the man standing a few feet away. The really large, gorgeous *scary* man. Who looked like he wanted to kill someone. I just hoped it wasn't me.

"Not sure Doc can fix this, boss. Probably gonna take an orthopedic surgeon."

"No. Nuh-uh." I tried to pull away but the arms holding me tightened and I groaned when Hardy accidentally jostled my arm as I moved. "I can't. Just wrap it or something. I can't go to the hospital. No insurance. No money. Have to work. Money. I need the money. Please. Please?"

I was crying. I could feel hot tears streaming down my cheeks. God, how did I get in this mess? My arm and wrist were totally screwed—which meant I was too. I couldn't do my routine with one hand. If I couldn't dance, I didn't get paid. Didn't get tips.

I figured out I was hyperventilating when Hardy shoved my head down and that voice in my ear ordered me to breathe again. Other voices penetrated over the noise of my panting.

"She had a knife. Lug Nut was bleeding."

The muscles behind me tensed like the guy holding me was going to toss me aside to go after that whiny voice. I didn't blame him. Then I heard the smack of a fist on skin. My stomach jolted and I winced. I knew that sound. Intimately. My old man had been a mean drunk before he took off for parts unknown, leaving my mom, older brother, me, and two little brothers behind.

"Fuck, Russki! What the hell was that for?"

Whiny Butt's mouth was back in action. I must have said something to that effect because the guy holding me chuckled. That laugh did all sorts of things to my insides, despite the fact I felt like I'd been hit by a train.

"She is wearing a fringed G-string. You have worked the door for two months yet you do not recognize her as one of our girls?" The Russian's voice raised goosebumps on my arms and I shivered. Which hurt. I whimpered.

"She had a knife. She could have been working for the fuckin' Hell Dogs."

"Get him out of my sight." I heard scuffling and then the Russian turned to stare at me. "Hollywood, you and Hardy will take her to hospital. I will have Doc meet you at the ER." He let out a disgruntled breath. "The police will have to question her. Lug Nut as well."

"No." I tried to pull away and black spots clouded my vision.

"Hold still, babe." The voice I couldn't see.

"I can't—"

"You will." There'd be no arguing with the Russian. "You will not have to pay. You belong to us. The Nightriders will pay."

Wait, what? I belonged to the Nightriders? No I didn't. I just worked for them. As a dancer. Besides, I had to make money. More money. And fast. "But I have to work. Please..." I turned to Hardy, begging him with my eyes. "Can't you just wrap it or splint it or something? I can go back to work. I can dance.

Just not the pole. Not for awhile. But I'm going back to work."

"No." I got hit with Dolby Surround Sound in triplicate.

The next thing I knew, I was in the arms of a guy—the as yet unseen Hollywood I figured—being carried out the back exit. A black Hummer was parked there. Hollywood simply slid into the back seat still holding me. How strong was this guy anyway? And then a blanket was tucked around me. That was good. I didn't know I was cold until I was covered up.

"Talk to me, babe." Hollywood's voice was sweet and low but it was still an order. "Why do you have to work?"

Hardy started driving. I didn't speak. I couldn't. I couldn't tell. If I did, something bad would happen to my mom. Maybe even my little brothers. My big brother was just like my dad. Dad was a drunk. Larry was a drug addict. Mom gambled.

"What do you need money for? You got kids or something?" Hollywood wasn't going to let this go.

"Or something," I muttered but he heard me.

"A man? You workin' to support some sonavabitch?"

I didn't like the ice creeping into his voice. Or his insinuation. Like I'd put up with a lazy bum? "Oh, hell no. It's my—" I clamped my mouth shut. Those men had been very explicit. I needed to pay them $5,000.00 a week for the next six months. If I told the cops, told anybody, they'd go after Mom and the boys.

"Your who?"

I shivered at his voice. "Nothing. Nobody."

"What's your name?"

"Name?" What? I felt like I was getting whiplash from the change of topic.

"Yes, your name. For when we get to the hospital."

"Oh." I mean, not like he'd personally want to know who I was or anything, right? He was just doing...what? Guard duty? Delivery service? "I'm Lainey. Lainey Walker."

"Well, Lainey Walker, I'm Hollywood."

"Um, okay. Hi, Hollywood."

His arms shifted me a little in his lap and I found my head tucked against his shoulder, my injured arm snugged carefully across my tummy. And...held in place by a splint and an Ace bandage. When had that happened? I didn't remember Hardy doing anything to me.

"What's gonna happen to Whiny Butt?" My voice was getting slurry.

I heard Hardy snicker. "Who?"

"Whiny Butt. Guy th'Russian hit?"

I caught the look Hardy exchanged with Hollywood through the rearview mirror. "You don't need to think about him, babe. It's being taken care of."

I wasn't sure I liked the implication, but I had another question. Maybe. If I could remember it. Oh, yeah. "Whassa hell dog?"

Hollywood started to say something then

cleared his throat before he spoke. "You don't need to worry about them either, babe."

"M'kay."

I think I dozed off—or passed out—because the next thing I knew, I was still sitting in Hollywood's lap only we were in a brightly-lit and very busy ER waiting room. I shifted position and whimpered. I felt a tremor run through Hollywood's body, like he was the one feeling pain. Weird. He nuzzled the top of my head and told me to try to sleep. My whole body throbbed and I didn't think I could, but the human body is funny. When pain gets really bad, everything sort of shuts down. I felt oddly safe so I quit fighting, closed my eyes, and passed out.

EIGHT

HOLLYWOOD

I WAS GOING fucking insane and it was just a matter of time before Hardy cold-cocked me as I paced by him. They'd finally taken Lainey back to an exam room. The nurse said something about X-rays. By then, Doc had arrived and he went to deal with the fucking ER doctor. Doc wasn't a Nightrider, but he was a hellava medico and he knew about us. Well, those of us who weren't quite human. We paid him big bucks to be on call 24/7 and he had a sweet clinic setup, financed by the club, that could handle one of us Wolves when we got too hurt to heal naturally, or any injury we needed to keep on the down low.

I kept compartmentalizing things. Part of me wanted to head back to the clubhouse and kill that fucking prospect. Whiny Butt. That's what Lainey had called him. Sounded like a good gawddamned road name for the asshole. The other part of me wanted to be in that fucking room with Lainey. The thought of another man touching her had my wolf tearing to get out.

The outer doors slid open and my wolf snarled, but I leashed him when I recognized Easy and his old lady, Sam. Easy was an enforcer for the Nightriders and Sam was good people. She'd been caught up in the Hell Dog bullshit not long ago and had almost died.

"I'll go get coffee for everyone," she offered and headed toward Vending.

Easy motioned me over and he, me n'Hardy huddled. "We might have a problem." He glanced at Hardy and the next thing I knew, they'd moved close.

My wolf was all kinds of snarly now. "What?"

"We talked to Hoss. This girl doesn't do privates."

I huffed out a relieved breath. Yeah, she was a dancer, but getting up close and personal in the private rooms was for other girls, not mine. I caught the scowl on Easy's face, like I'd totally missed his point. "What?"

"She doesn't do privates." He iterated each word. "Hasn't ever done one. Why was she doing one for Lug Nut?"

Fuck. Now I caught what I'd overlooked. Yeah. Something wasn't right.

"This whole thing is fucked up." Hardy kept one eye on the exit. "How did those assholes get into the club? And why go after Lug?"

"Maybe the girl was the target?" None of us had heard Sam walk up. She passed out cups of hot, black coffee.

"Why would the Hell Dogs go after her?"

Hardy asked Sam, beating me to the question.

"Especially since she doesn't know what the fuck they are." That got three sets of eyes staring at me. "She asked me, in the Hummer, right before she passed out. Wanted to know what a hell dog was."

I didn't like the look passing between Easy and Hardy. Doc pushed through the swinging doors between us and the exam rooms. I liked the expression on his face even less.

"Somebody did a number on her wrist. Every bone, including distal ulna and radius bone fractures. I won't give you the medical mumbo jumbo. Just believe me when I say she's messed up. The ortho is taking her up to surgery. If she's lucky, he can do a plate and screws instead of an external fixator. She'll have mostly full function back in a year."

"A year?" Sam gulped. "For a broken wrist?"

Easy shook his head but Hardy growled at her. "He crushed her fucking wrist."

Sam's eyes widened. "One of the Hell Dogs?"

"No. One of us." I gave Easy a side look and he read my intent easy enough.

"Russki's dealing, Wood. You need to calm the fuck down."

Doc cleared his throat. "The good news, if there is any in all of this, is that she'll be out of things the rest of the night. Cops won't be able to talk to her until tomorrow. Everybody should just go home. Let her family deal with her."

My wolf didn't like that idea, not one fucking bit. Have to admit, I wasn't too thrilled either. "I'm stayin'."

"You aren't next of kin." Doc inhaled to give his standard lecture on the facts of hospital life.

"Says who?" The fuckers here didn't know anything about her. Or me. I was stayin' until she was awake and I knew she was breathing. My wolf liked that idea a hellava lot.

Figuring he couldn't talk me out of it, Doc nodded and went back into the inner ER sanctum to tell them about me. Sam looked like she wanted to stay but she and Easy had two kids depending on them. "Get on home. All of you. Though if someone can bring my bike—"

"Already done, brother." Easy handed me the keys. "Sam brought her Jeep. She can take me back to the clubhouse then head home."

I could tell that decree didn't sit well with Sam, but this was club business. She'd been Easy's mate long enough to have that figured out.

"Thanks for the coffee, Sam."

"Keep us posted." Hardy patted my shoulder and I nodded.

They cleared out and a few minutes later, Doc introduced me to a nurse and she led me to a waiting area deeper in the hospital, close to the operating rooms. I didn't relax, all but jumping to my feet every time someone came or went. By three, when no one from her family had showed, I called Hoss to ask.

"Finally got a call answered. By her little brother. What the hell a kid was doing awake at midnight, I don't know. He had to relay messages to his mother. The old bitch said she was too busy to deal with Lainey. The kid, Levi, was crying. Asked if we'd take care of her, make sure she was safe from the bad men. The mother cut off the call before I could get any more info."

"Fuck, Hoss." My brain immediately went down a dark path. Bad men were after Lainey? Maybe she *had* been the target. Or maybe, she was working with the Hell Dogs. Either way, I'd find out as soon as she was awake enough to talk.

"Yeah, something's rotten there, Wood. The club needs t'look into it. She's not the type of girl we normally get workin' here. I'll check with the other dancers, see what they know about her."

"Keep me in the loop, and Digger will need to be updated."

I ended the call and gave up. My wolf was so upset I had to pace to keep him under control. Deep didn't even come close to describing the shit that was raining down on the club.

About ten minutes later, a tired looking guy in rumpled scrubs appeared. "You here for Lainey Walker?"

Since I was the only person in the room, it

didn't take a genius to figure that out. "Yeah."

"Good news and bad news. Do you want the technical explanation?"

"No. Give that to Doc Carson. He'll distill it down."

The doctor gave me the once-over, eying the patches on my cut, my tats, and the glint in my eye.

"Is she your..." He paused as if choosing the next word carefully.

"She's mine. Yeah." His face went hard as he made the wrong assumptions. Pissed me off he thought I'd hurt her, but I was glad he cared. "Wasn't me, Doc. There was an incident at the club. She got caught in the middle." He arched a brow, waiting for more. I gave it to him. "The one who laid hands on her? Yeah, that won't happen again."

"Okay, then. The graze on her face was minor. She might need a little plastic surgery. I had a colleague take a look while I was working on her wrist and arm." The doctor rubbed one hand over the crown of his head, nudging off the scrub cap. As if surprised he'd brushed it off, he stared at the scrap of material for a few moments. Then he spoke. "That graze was from a large caliber bullet. She's lucky to be alive."

My wolf was pacing, stiff-legged and pissed, just below the surface of my skin. Part of me wondered why we had such a vested interest in the girl but the rest of me felt exactly the same.

"You don't gotta tell me. We got there a heartbeat after the fuckin' gun went off."

"She wasn't so lucky with the wrist and arm. Your girl is in good shape. Strong bones. That'll help. She's healthy."

I caught the speculation. "Just because she dances at Chasin' Tail, don't mean she's a druggie."

"Understood. She's not. No trace of drugs or alcohol in her tox screen. But someone—" The doctor looked speculative again. "—did a real number on her arm."

Fuckin' Whiny Butt was a Wolf. He'd twisted the knife out of her hand then stomped her arm and wrist, grinding her bones into the floor. The doctor's eyes widened and he backed up three steps. I forced the wolf deep and didn't quite meet the man's gaze. Pretty fuckin' sure too damn much feral was leakin' out.

"Sorry. Pissed off she's hurt. Pissed off someone else is dealin' with the asshole, but I need to be here."

The doctor exhaled, relaxing some. "I can tell you care about her. Her immediate recovery is fairly simple, but that arm will need months of rehab, perhaps even more surgery. There's no insurance."

"She's covered." He started to speak again and I cut him off. "She belongs to the Nightriders. We take care of our own. Her bills will be paid."

"I don't pretend to understand your lifestyle but I do believe you'll take care of her.

She has a long way to go to heal."

"When can I see her?"

"She's being moved to recovery. We'll monitor her for an hour or so before moving her to a room."

"Private."

"Excuse me?"

"I want her in a private room."

"You realize the expense—"

"Just do it. Money isn't an issue." It wasn't, and her security was. There was something wrong about tonight's attack and about Lainey's role in it. Until we figured out what, I was sticking close to her. Satisfied with that decision, my wolf settled down.

"As you wish. I'll make the arrangements. A nurse will find you here when Ms. Walker is moved to her room."

"Thanks, doctor." I didn't offer him my hand. He didn't offer his.

NINE

HOLLYWOOD

MY WOLF KNEW there was an intruder before I did. I came up out of the chair, teeth bared and claws barely sheathed. The guy in the suit standing just inside the door was a Wolf. He also had a holstered gun and when his jacket moved, a bright, shiny badge stuck on his belt. Fuck. A Wolf cop. I wondered if the Russian knew.

Lainey was finally sleeping. She'd come out of recovery about five a.m. I fell asleep about seven, after the doctor checked her again. He'd been optimistic about her getting full range of motion and mentioned her muscle tone again. He knew she was a dancer at Tail's. I don't think he was too impressed. Or hell, he might have seen her there and was as impressed as hell. I didn't make it into the club very often. I had other things I did for the Nightriders, but the one time I'd watched her? Oh, fucking yeah, she could work that pole.

Once I leashed my wolf, and evidently the cop did the same with his, we glared at each other. I motioned for him to step back into the hall. He stared and postured—fuckin' alpha Wolf shit—but I was an alpha too so I didn't back down.

"She's asleep," I growled softly at him. "I don't want her disturbed."

He held up his hands at that and backed out. I followed, and partially closed the door behind me. If Lainey woke up, I'd be at her side in a flash. Crossing my arms over my chest, I leaned a shoulder against the door jamb and stared at the cop. He stared back.

After a long stand-off, he reached in his hip pocket and pulled out an ID case. He flashed it. "Derek Alexander, Homeland Security."

DHS? What the fuck? I continued the stare down.

"What happened last night?"

"Don't see how Homeland has any interest in a fight in a strip joint."

"Homeland has interests in a lot of different things."

I could see he was thinking things over, debating where to take the conversation next. I didn't move, waiting patiently. I was a Wolf. He might be a Wolf, too, but he was the interloper in my territory. I was the predator. He was prey.

"Look at it this way, the enemy of your enemy could just be your friend."

Snorting, I uncrossed my arms and hooked my thumbs in my belt. "Yeah? And who would be the enemy and who would be the friend?"

"Hell Dogs and me."

Okay, he had my attention now. I wouldn't walk across the street to piss on a Hell Dog if he was on fire and felt that way before they'd kidnapped two Nightrider old ladies. We'd already had a feud goin' before Wolf DNA and some dark government crap got tossed into the mix and made things worse. A few months prior to the kidnappings, a former Army SpecOps guy dropped by. Mac McIntire's old man had been the Nightriders' national prez before the Russian took him out during a Blood Moon, claiming the MC. Even now, Brick McIntire's hide was nailed to the clubhouse wall.

We'd figured the former soldier had been there to demand retribution. Turned out, there was no blood lost between him and his old man. He'd stopped by to warn us—and wanted Russski to put the word out to all the chapters. Black Root. That's the name of the shady corporation working with the government— and the Hell Dogs were workin' for them. They'd kidnapped kids. Killed our kind. And now a government agent was standing here telling me he was interested in the Dogs.

I was about to dig deeper when the fed stiffened and stepped away so he could keep an eye on me and the corridor at the same time. I felt the power about half a second after he moved. The Russian. I was used to the air going all still like before a storm. Happened every time Russski got pissed off. Like he was now.

Russki stalked down the hallway, waves of energy sparking around him. Other people immediately moved out of his way. He stopped in front of us and I'll give the fed this, he didn't back away while the boss gave him the once over.

Without taking his eyes off Alexander, the Russian acknowledged me. "Hollywood."

"Russki."

"Who is your friend?"

"Funny you should ask, boss. We were just discussing strange friendships." The Russian arched a brow and damn if he didn't look like a tsar or something. I could see the effect on the fed, but I hid my grin as I made introductions. "Derek Alexander. Department of Homeland Security."

"And you would be Sergei Rusakovavich, national president of the Nightriders," the fed said.

I faded back, still blocking the door to Lainey's room but keeping an ear open for any noise from inside. I had no part of this conversation, except to back up Russki.

"Why are you here?" The boss didn't beat around the bush.

The fed didn't pussyfoot either. "Your girl was attacked by the Hell Dogs."

"Was she?"

"I want to know why."

"I wish to know this information as well. What interest do you have in the Hell Dogs?"

Alexander glanced up and down the

hallway, his lips pursed as he considered the question. I could almost see the wheels turning in his head. He knew shit. The question was, how much shit would he share? And how much shit would we catch for knowing?

"Let's just say they've been on my radar for awhile. They are in bed with some people who—"

Someone screamed. Lainey! I was at her bedside a blink later, scooping her into my arms. I had my hands full soothing her, but I noticed Russki standing in the doorway blocking the fed from entering. Good. My wolf was already going nuts. He'd go rabid if a strange Wolf got close to my mate.

Wait. What the fuck? My wolf nosed me, assuring me of the fact that Lainey belonged to us.

"Moonstruck?"

"So it appears."

Alexander's and the Russian's voices washed over me as I stroked Lainey's hair back from her face. I didn't pay them much attention.

"Shhh, baby. I'm here. You aren't alone. You'll be all right."

"Promise?" Her shaky voice was muffled against my chest.

"Promise."

"Okay." She tilted her head back just enough to look at me. "Just one thing."

"Yeah, darlin'."

"Who are you?"

TEN

LAINEY

"I'M HOLLYWOOD."

I went to wipe the crud stuck to my eyelashes and realized I couldn't really move my right arm. My brain whirled like that little rainbow icon on a computer screen, spinning and spinning and spinning. I glanced around. Hospital. Broken arm. A man. A fight. Lug Nut. Private dance. Chasin' Tail. Details fell into place.

My heart rate kicked up and the machine beside my bed beeped ominously. Then the pain washed over me again. My vision blacked out and white prickles danced across the darkness.

"Lainey?" That voice sounded far away. Who was calling me?

"Babe?" Oh. Yeah. Hollywood.

Warm hands eased me back against the pillow. More voices echoed from the shadows.

"What is wrong with her?"

"I don't know, Russki!"

"What did you do to her?"

"Back off, asshole."

"Give me room. I've notified the on-call resident. I need to check her vitals." A woman's voice, no-nonsense and calm. "Everybody out."

"Fuck that shit. I'm stayin'."

"Are you family?"

"Damn straight I am." Hollywood again. Wait. He wasn't family. Where was my mom? Oh no! Who was looking after my little brothers? I clawed my way through the agonizing pain, found a speck of light and homed in on it.

"Easy, Lainey. Breathe, baby. Just breathe. I've got you."

Something burned in my arm, shooting into my bloodstream.

"I've given her a sedative." A different male voice. "The surgeon said she could have a morphine drip if she needs one. I'll order it."

"No." Hollywood again. I wanted him to shut up. Morphine sounded really, *really* good at the moment.

I opened my eyes and focused on his face. Whatever drug they'd given me through the IV made me feel all floaty and a little bit drunk. At least the pain was easing back. I swallowed down the last of the bile, managed a deep breath.

"You're pretty."

A quick grin. "Yeah, I am."

Oh, Hollywood was a devil. I'd have to be very careful…wait. I'd said that out loud? Well…shoot.

"Shhh, Lainey. Go back to sleep, darlin'. I'm

here. Not goin' anywhere. You're safe."

Safe. Now that was a concept that had eluded me lately. I hadn't felt safe in a long, long time. Except here, in a hospital—a place I loathed—a man who was a complete stranger but who didn't feel like a stranger sitting next to me, and throbbing agony beyond anything my father had ever heaped on me, I did. Feel safe.

I'd seen Hollywood somewhere before and I felt like I should know more about him. I tried to keep my eyes open so I could think but they wouldn't cooperate. Warm lips on my forehead. Scruffy shadow beard scraping my temple. Strong fingers holding mine gently, a thumb rubbing across the back of my hand. I breathed deeply and smiled. He smelled of baking bread and mesquite smoke. Weird. I'd sort it out later. Yes. Later...

🐾 🐾 🐾 🐾

HOLLYWOOD

I WATCHED LAINEY settle into sleep. Her face remained pale and drawn. Pain fuckin' radiated off her. I'd absorb all of it if I could. It was killin' me to watch her like this.

"A morphine pump is a perfectly acceptable pain management tool."

That prick of a doctor studied the chart in his hands. No. He was only a resident. Young. Cocky. Fuck him. "No morphine. No oxy."

"I don't believe you have the right to make those decisions."

"I believe you'd be wrong. There's a history of addiction in her family." Gravedigger had done some digging and texted me. Her brother was a meth head and her mother spent most of her time gambling. No father in the picture, only twin brothers who were younger. She looked after them.

After Hoss's call, Digger tracked down Lainey's mother. Nobody was home. Sunday fucking morning and the old bitch was at a casino. Digger had to drag the woman off the floor, her complaining the whole time. Digger told her to get her ass home to look after her own kids. When she told him the boys were in her car out in the parking lot, he'd lost his shit.

Dig called for backup. Lainey's little brothers were currently staying with Sam and Easy. Their adopted son, Jonah, was about the same age so that was good. Less for Lainey to worry about when she woke up again.

The doctor *tsked* at me. I crossed my arms over my chest. The pussy's face drained of color. "Fine. But she doesn't have to be in pain." He scribbled on the chart, dropped it into the rack on the foot of her bed, and left. Good riddance.

I sat down in the chair I'd pulled up next to the bed and took her uninjured hand in mine. She stirred slightly, mumbling something. After a sigh, she sank deeper into sleep.

A light tap on the door, followed by it

swinging open, brought me halfway to my feet. If that damn doctor was back… Wizard stuck his head in and I relaxed.

"I'll sit with her," he whispered. "The Russian and Easy need to talk to you."

"Where?"

Wiz jerked his head toward the window. "They're outside. Go on down. Get some food, fresh air. She's safe with me."

My wolf didn't like the idea. Wiz indicated a chair in the far corner. "I'll sit over there. Won't touch her."

Okay, that was just weird. Wiz tended to adopt some of the dancers—in a brother-protector kind of way but to tell me he'd stay hands off? I gave him a look and he laughed.

"Clueless sonavabitch."

I snarled at that.

"Your reactions to her? Remind you of anyone?"

Scowling, I stared at him, glanced to Lainey's sleeping face then back to him.

"Easy? When he first met Sam?" Wiz hinted.

What the fuck? That was bullshit. My wolf got all smug. *Mine*. No, she wasn't. *Ours*, the damn critter insisted. Holy fuck. "I am not fuckin' moonstruck."

Wizard laughed in my face and clapped his hand over his mouth to smother the sound. "You so fuckin' are, brother. Now get your ass downstairs before the Russian comes hunting for both our hides."

He had a point. My wolf still didn't like the idea of leaving Lainey, but Wiz snagged me around the neck with his arm. "She's yours, bro. I'll protect her."

His words settled both my wolf and me, enough so we could leave Lainey alone with another man—another Wolf. I still dragged my feet and it took every bit of my will to shut the door behind me. I could trust Wiz. He was a Nightrider brother.

I found the Russian, Easy, and Hoss in the parking lot, leaning against their Harleys. I didn't like the looks on their faces. Not one damn bit.

"Deadhead called," Easy said. "That motel clerk?"

I tilted my head, waiting for him to continue.

"She's dead."

ELEVEN

HOLLYWOOD

THE RUSSIAN'S EYES FLARED. "She was murdered." The words hung frozen in the air.

"The Hell Dog who got away?" The question was a shot in the dark but it was the first thought I had. We hadn't been able to track him so maybe he'd just gone to ground in Topeka.

"Don't know. Digger's tryin' to find out." Easy glanced at the Russian. "When Deadhead got word, he went down to the scene but he couldn't get much info."

We'd given the clerk protection and she'd been killed. We couldn't prove it was Hell Dogs but it didn't take much of a leap to point the finger. I was bone-deep angry. I'd done the background check on her. She'd been a nice girl. Working to pay her way through community college.

"What happened?"

Easy rubbed the back of his neck, staring down at his boots. "Parking lot on campus. She was snatched after a late class. Security located her car the next morning when she didn't show up for work. Bastards dumped her a block from the cop shop about an hour after her car was found."

"Wizard hacked into the ME's database." Hoss continued the story. "At least they just executed her. Double tap to the head. No rape. That's not much, but it's something."

"Yeah." Two things Nightriders didn't do—hurt kids or rape. Everybody else? No boundaries.

"There's something else." Now Hoss was staring at his boots.

"What?"

"Lainey."

"What about her?"

"She doesn't do privates, Hollywood. Not until last night."

Well, fuck. Suspicion was plastered all over their faces. "I'll talk to her."

"When?"

Easy asked the question, but it was the Russian staring past me back toward the hospital that captured my attention. I glanced around. Cops. Two of them in uniform and one in a suit. Fuck. Officer Gerald and his sidekick, along with the fed. Russki was stride-for-stride with me as we headed inside.

By the time we got to Lainey's room, Wiz was in handcuffs. Gerald was all puffed up with ego, the fed looked pissed, and the other uniform just stood off to one side, his hand on the butt of his pistol, glaring at anyone who looked in his direction.

"You got a warrant?" I tried to sound cool instead of pissed. Didn't exactly work.

Gerald whirled around. "You!"

"You wanna take those cuffs off my boy there, slick?"

"I got another pair here with your name on 'em, *slick*." Gerald got right up in my face. "We're taking the bitch into protective custody."

The fed stepped between us, a good thing for the cop. I was ready to rip his throat out.

The Russian smiled. I backed out of the way. I knew that smile. It usually meant someone was going to die.

"There is no reason for anyone in law enforcement to take the girl."

"There is. It's necessary for her safety." The fed was dumber than I'd given him credit for.

🐾 🐾 🐾 🐾

LAINEY

COMING AWAKE FROM a drug-induced sleep, I heard voices out in the hallway. All male. I strained to hear what they were saying after I identified Hollywood's voice and that of the Russian's. That man still scared me spitless. The other guys I didn't recognize.

"Necessary for safety." A stranger's voice.

Safety? Whose? I almost squeaked in my fear.

"She belongs to the Nightriders. We take

care of Lainey just as we will deal with this situation." The Russian.

Well that answered my question. Me. My safety. I pulled the covers up to my chin as if I could hide from everything going on in my batshit crazy life.

"You don't understand." The stranger again. "The investigation—"

"*You* don't understand." Hollywood's voice was barely discernible beneath his growl.

I heard a body hit something solid—like a wall—then snarls and growls.

"We have no fight with Homeland Security." The Russian, sounding…almost reasonable. "Hollywood has claimed her. Do what you must, but be aware that we take care of our own. She stays with us. Do your investigation. Arrest the ones who did this, but be warned. If you wish to take them to trial, arrest them before *we* find them."

"Dammit. I've spent years tracking these assholes." The stranger who was with Homeland Security. "Your girl isn't the only one they've hurt."

I heard more snarls and another thud.

"Enough, Hollywood. Go inside." That was the Russian's do-it-or-die voice. I'd heard it the night I got hurt.

A moment later, the door slammed open, bouncing off the wall, and Hollywood stalked in. I just thought I'd been scared before. He looked like a big, bad wolf straight out of Red Riding Hood's nightmares. He took one look at me and his face morphed into a stricken expression before the anger surged back. He shut the door, faced me.

"Don't fucking cry. If you cry, I'll rip out his throat."

None of this made sense. My life was so completely out of control and now I was caught between an outlaw motorcycle gang and freaking Homeland Security. One tear slid down my cheek. I couldn't help it.

"Ah, babe," he groaned. Then I was in his arms and everything was okay. Which was totally insane.

🐾 🐾 🐾 🐾

RUSSKI

ALEXANDER MOTIONED FOR the officer Hollywood called Gerald to remove the handcuffs from Wizard. There was history there—between the cop and Wood. My curiosity would be satisfied another time. Wiz hooked his thumbs in the pockets of his jeans and leaned against the wall, booted feet crossed at the ankles—a still-life sketch titled Indolent Thug. The agent remained a buffer between us and the police.

"If Miss Walker is awake, I need to question her." His eyes met mine, but he lowered his gaze for a moment. Good. He understood who held the power.

"Screw this." Gerald surged past

Alexander. "I'm taking the bitch."

The cop did not reach the door. The fed put a hand on the idiot's shoulder. Gerald squirmed, wincing when the DHS agent squeezed, but he stood silent. It would have made no difference if Alexander had refrained from intervening. Wizard blocked the door. I glanced at the second officer—the one who had remained silent and aloof during this confrontation. He watched intently, had seen how fast both Wizard and the fed had moved. This cop wasn't surprised. Interesting.

Once upon a time only a very few select humans knew about our kind. Most considered Wolves to be the stuff of myth, or fiction. Unlike the way we are portrayed in the cinema or literature, we are not werewolves. We are *Lupi versi pellis.* Wolf shifters. Our bite will not turn a human. The ability to connect to our wolves and change into their shape is coded in our DNA.

For centuries, we lived in isolated packs, though there were those who served kings and generals down through the ages. In the dark times, Wolves were hunted almost to extinction. Our birth rate and the survival of our young has always been a tenuous thing. Now, to discover knowledge of our existence was becoming more prevalent troubled me. The message Mac McIntire brought to us several months ago was hitting too close to home.

I did not trust anyone from the government

or law enforcement. Those in power had never earned it. From my earliest recollections, I—and others like me—had been tools for the powerful. No more. Now I had the power and I would protect the Nightriders and those who belonged to us.

Odors thickened the air. Sulfur wafted from Agent Alexander. The man was frustrated and his nose was wrinkled from the stench of stale beer and puke pouring from Gerald. The angry cop was disgusted. I shifted my gaze to the second officer. My nose sifted through the scents. Yes, there. An aroma rich and yeasty, with a sharp bite, like malt vinegar. Anticipation. Curiouser and curiouser.

"Agent Alexander, we will make Miss Walker available to you another time, when she is feeling better. In the meantime, I will arrange for you to interview the man who was also attacked in this incident. Will that suffice for now?"

The fed wisely moved Gerald away from the door. "Yes." He reached into the breast pocket of his suit coat and presented me with his card. "Call me when I can question him." He forcibly turned Gerald away from Lainey's door. "Let's go."

Alexander ushered the two local cops down the hall, Gerald cussing and arguing, the other man walking silently. All three boarded the elevator and the silent cop's poker face wavered for one moment—when he stared straight at me and offered a knowing smirk.

It was always the silent ones who were most deadly. "Wizard."

"Boss?"

"Doc should arrange the girl's release. Wood will stay with her."

"Done."

He was already speaking into his phone as I pulled out my own and dialed. "Easy, I have a job for you."

TWELVE

I SNIFFLED AND pushed back from Wood. I just…Hollywood? Seriously? I couldn't call him that. "May I ask you something personal?"

His thumbs brushed across my cheeks, wiping the last of my tears. "Sure, babe."

"Hollywood isn't your real name." I waited for him to reply but he just stared at me. "What?"

"What what?"

Totally confused I made one of those comical WTF faces.

He continued. "The only question you asked was *what.*"

"Seriously?" Why did I always get the literal ones. "Fine. Your real name isn't Hollywood, is it?"

"Yes and no."

I seconded my WTF face. "What does that even mean?"

He smiled and my gaze dropped to his mouth. A rich chuckle rolled over me and I thought of gooey-hot brownies straight from the oven. The man was far too sexy for my own good. In the find-a-good-man contest, I was a total loser.

"My road name is Hollywood."

"Oh! I know what that is. Sort of. It's like special nickname or something, right?"

"Yeah. Or something. When a member patches in, the brothers give him the name. It becomes who we are. What each of us is."

"So what's your real name?"

"Hollywood."

I threw up my hands and almost screamed as my right arm barely moved. Greasy waves of pain swamped me and I closed my eyes against the swarming black dots clouding my vision.

"Shhh, baby. Shhh. Lie back."

Warm lips kissed my forehead as Hollywood's arms eased me back against the raised hospital bed. He fidgeted with the pillow and when the pain eased off enough I could open my eyes, his worried gaze slammed into me.

"I'm sorry."

Okay, color me confused again. "About what?"

"I shouldn't tease you. At least not until you've healed."

My breath caught and I forced my lungs to expand. The doctors were talking about long-term recovery. Did that mean Hollywood planned to stick around? Why? Why would he do that? Bits and pieces of conversation filtered back into my consciousness. *She belongs to us. To the Nightriders. We take care of our own. He has claimed her.* None of it made much sense.

"Hilton."

I blinked, refocused my attention on Hollywood. "Excuse me?"

"My name. Eric Hilton."

"Are you—"

"No. No relation." He shrugged. "I get that question a lot. My mother was an orphan in the system so she picked out a last name she thought sounded classy. She didn't know my father's last name."

I chewed that over for awhile. "May I ask another personal question?"

One corner of his mouth curled into a wry...snarl. "Babe, Twenty Questions works both ways."

Ouch. He had me there. I'd always been far too curious for my own good, but I wanted to know more about him. A lot more. I didn't know why, just that there was a driving need—almost a compulsion—to find out. "Okay."

"My turn then. Why are you dancing at Chasin' Tail?"

I glanced at my right arm then flicked my left hand in a motion to encompass the medical equipment in the room. "I'm not dancing now."

His eyes narrowed and that snarl grew more pronounced. I jumped in before he could call me on my non-answer. "My turn. Your mom didn't know your father's name so were you like...what? A one-night stand, a..." I paused. Had his mother been raped or something horrible? It was none of my business so I just let the rest of my thought trail off.

"He never told her his last name. Then he was arrested. Sent to prison. He died there before I was born."

The tone of his voice never changed. There was a story there, one I desperately wanted to know but figured I'd be pushing my luck to ask now. "Okay. Your turn."

"Why haven't you asked about your family?"

My family? My heart started pounding. The twins! "My brothers! Oh, nonono." I threw the covers off, tried to get out of the bed, but Hollywood's big hand slapped against my chest and held me in place.

"Easy, cowgirl."

"No, no. You don't understand. My mother...she..."

"She what?"

"She...gambles. She forgets the time. The boys. I have to take—"

"They're covered, babe."

"I...wait. What?"

"After you got hurt. One of the brothers went to find her after Hoss called your house."

Guilt washed over me. Had someone been inside, seen how we lived? I swallowed the saliva pooling in my mouth.

"Gravedigger tracked her down at the

casino."

Wait…Gravedigger? I…did not want to know why he was called that. "Levi and Louie?"

"Locked in her car in the parking lot." His voice had ice crystals in it. "They're taken care of."

Taken care of? By who? This Gravedigger person? Were they okay? "What does that mean?" My question was almost lost in the whoosh of the nervous breath I inhaled.

"Easy and his old lady. Sam has two kids. Jonah's the same age as your brothers. They're staying there 'til we get things squared away."

"We? *We* who?"

"Us, babe. The brothers. The Nightriders. You belong to us now."

The door opened before I could argue that. A man who looked to be in his forties and wearing worn jeans, a T-shirt featuring a grim reaper figure, and a stethoscope around his neck slouched in.

"Doc."

"Hollywood." The guy stared at me. "Paperwork is started. The Russian wants her released to you."

"Figured." Hollywood raised his chin to indicate the other man. "Lainey, Doc Carson."

"Is he a real doctor?" I didn't mean to say that aloud, but looking at him? I had my doubts. Both of them laughed at me.

"Have the paper from John Hopkins Medical School and everything." He grabbed my chart and fanned through the pages, skimming the information. "You got lucky, girl. I know your orthopedic surgeon. He does great work. Do your rehab right, you might be back to full functionality in less than a year."

I froze. I didn't have a year. I had...less than six months. I had less than a week. I had... I couldn't breathe.

"Damn, girl."

"What's wrong with her?"

The doctor and Hollywood. They were talking. Moving. Touching me but I could barely feel them. I forced my brain to remember, to calculate. What day was it? I needed five thousand dollars like...now.

"She's not breathin', Doc." Hollywood sounded panicked.

"She's hyperventilating. Move, Wood."

The next thing I knew, I was sitting in the chair normally occupied by Hollywood, my knees spread and my head between them. Warm fingers curled around my calves and I cringed a little. I hadn't shaved in...well, however long I'd been in the hospital.

"Breathe for me, baby." Hollywood's voice was calm but laced with urgency. "Deep breath in. Hold it. Deep breath out." He was breathing that way and it seemed deceptively simple to follow his lead.

A few minutes later, I was breathing normally. I raised my head, my gaze crashing into brown eyes the color of burnt umber. I remembered the shade from my crayon box.

Burnt umber. It sounded so classy for a scorched shade of brown. Sexy. And looking into Hollywood's eyes, I realized there was so much more to that color.

"Christ, baby. Keep lookin' at me like that and I'll fuck you here and now."

Fuck me? As in...he wanted to *fuck* me? The girls perked right up at that thought and the ache in my arm dropped to a spot between my thighs and started to throb. I licked my lips and judging by the expression on Hollywood's face, that was so not what I should have done.

"You're killin' me, Lainey." His face was stark, almost as if he was the one in pain. "Get her off of all this medical crap, Doc, and deal with the paperwork. I'm takin' her home. Now."

THIRTEEN

HOLLYWOOD

I DIDN'T WAIT for a wheelchair, a nurse, none of that shit. I wrapped Lainey in the blanket I stripped off the hospital bed, gathered her into my arms and headed out as soon as Doc got her unhooked. My dick was so fucking hard it felt like it would break off with each step I took. I didn't care about that either. I only knew one thing—I had to get her away, get her alone, and I was going to fuck her until we were done.

Somebody was laughing—Doc, I think. Didn't matter. He was keeping the hospital people away from us. I took her out through the ER department. As the automatic doors slithered open, the MC's Hummer pulled up, Hardy at the wheel.

Yeah, duh. Would have been a bitch getting Lainey home on my bike. The back passenger door popped open and Sandhog jumped out. Sandy was one of the human members of the club. His old man had been a Wolf but the *lupi* gene skipped Sandhog. I could slide into the seat he'd just vacated, my girl still in my arms.

Two pairs of eyes—Hardy's and Wizard's—met mine via the rear view mirror. Hardy was the one who spoke. "Your place?"

"Yeah." I tossed my keys to Sandy. He'd get my bike home.

I should have had them take us to the Nightrider compound. There were too many unanswered questions about Lainey's safety, but I didn't want her around any of the brothers. Just having Hardy and Wizard in the front seat was doing a number on my wolf. He was ready to rip throats. And fuck. He really wanted me to fuck Lainey, fuck and claim her.

Workin' on it, I told him. He growled back something that sounded like, *About time.*

My apartment was pretty bare. It was a place to crash when I wasn't at the compound, but I had a California king, with clean sheets, beer in the fridge, and a big screen. Good enough. And it wasn't like I brought bitches here to fuck. Just Lainey. And she damn sure was *not* a bitch. Hardy helped me get her inside then he disappeared. I knew Wizard'd be close. My brothers knew their shit—knew my shit.

I was fucking moonstruck and until I had my dick buried in Lainey's sweet pussy I'd be a crazy sonavabitch—insane enough I wasn't going to tell her what I was, what was happening. She was my mate. *Our* mate. I wouldn't give her a chance to turn me down because if she did, I'd go apeshit and people would die.

There'd always been that part of me—the part I held leashed tight. My sire had been a Nightrider. And a Wolf. One of Brick McIntire's lieutenants. He'd taken one look at my mom, followed her home to the foster family who put a roof over her head, and he'd claimed her. She'd been seventeen—her chronological age. In her soul? She was a hundred. His name was Rooster. That's all she knew, all she cared about. They never married, even though they were together almost five years. He got busted running guns, tried, convicted, and he died three months into a ten-year sentence, murdered by a crew of Hell Dogs.

Brick and Lug Nut showed up on the doorstep right before I turned twelve. Right after Officer Douglas Gerald moved in on my mom. He beat the crap out of me one night, left me bleeding and unconscious. I guess Mom called the club. All I know is, they showed up, Gerald was gone, and Mom died soon after. The Nightriders raised me after that.

And now I understood. I understood why Mom struggled to be a decent mother, to make me cookies and shit. Deep down, she didn't care about anything but my old man. They'd been mated. I got that now. Fuck. How had she lived without him? I'd eat a bullet if I ever lost Lainey. Maybe things would smooth out once she was mine, once she knew we were mates.

I set her down on the bed. Her skin was flushed, her eyes—how the hell had I not noticed they were the color of a summer sky? Blue. So fucking blue they mirrored my reflection. Fuck. I looked hungry. Desperate. Yeah. I was both of those things. But Lainey was my mate. I had to take care of her. *Love* her.

Breathing hard, I knelt beside her, took her hands. "I'm going to make love to you, Lainey. I'm going to do my damnedest to be gentle. You're hurt. I know that. I don't want to hurt you more. Fuck, I think I'd kill myself if I did, but if I'm not inside you, fucking you, soon—" I stopped. I needed to tell her. I couldn't not tell her what the deal was.

"Shhh." She hushed me with a finger across my lips, but she was soft doin' it. "This is crazy. You're crazy. I'm crazy. It's okay. I want this...want you." She giggled softly. "Maybe it's the pain killers. I don't know. I just know I want you to kiss me, and I want to get out of this dumb hospital gown." She reached up, tried to find the ties on the back of that ugly gown.

"Let me. Please." I leaned in, pushing between her thighs and trailed a fingertip along the golden skin covering her collar bone. "Let me."

Her eyes were shy but her smile teasing. "Go for it."

I found the top tie. Tugged. The cotton slipped off her shoulders and I all but swallowed my tongue. I forgot about keeping her safe. I forgot about explaining her new reality. I forgot about everything but the reality of her, here and now. The texture of her skin, smooth, soft, like trailing my fingers over a new leaf. The rich scent of her arousal—almonds and coffee. The sizzling, ripe taste of her that echoed her lust when I took her mouth, my tongue claiming her.

She surrounded me—her scent, her taste, the textures of her skin and lips until they were—she was—everything. My entire world had narrowed to this woman. She was everything I never dared imagine, everything I could ever want or need.

I touched the cast on her arm, jerked back. This was wrong. Taking her now, when she was injured, when she didn't know what I was—it was a mistake, and edged very close to stepping over the line. I tried to stop, but her good hand clenched in my T-shirt pulling me back to her. No way could I stop. I couldn't chance her leaving me. Later, I promised both of us. I'd tell her everything later, when she knew me, knew who I was instead of what I was.

I tugged the shapeless gown away from her shoulders, baring her to me. I sat back on my heels and just looked at her. She moved to cover her breasts, but I stopped her, snagging her hand and holding it against her thigh with my own.

"Don't," I growled. I could barely speak, my humanity leaking away as my need ballooned. But I needed to. I needed to give her words.

"Tryin' to think of something romantic to say, but it's really hard when all the blood's drained out of my head."

"Um. Okay." She blushed, and her nipples turned rosy. Fuck.

"You are beautiful. Just fuckin' beautiful."

Leaning forward again, I set my teeth on her flesh. Her head fell back and I grazed my way up her chest to the hollow beneath her chin where her pulse throbbed. I felt her breath hitch as I cupped one breast, swallowed her moan as I kissed her again.

I had to come up for air. "We might need oxygen before we're done."

She laughed and my dick throbbed in time with the sound. "I figure we might need a fire extinguisher. I'm about to self-combust."

"I'll make sure you do."

"Promises, promises."

I grinned. "I am seriously crazy about you." I licked one nipple then the other, loved the sound of her choked gasp for air. "I think you need to lay down, cowgirl."

"Not yet." She reached out and grabbed the hem of my T-shirt. "I like the way you look at me. I did right from the first time you walked into Chasin' Tail."

"You saw me?"

"Yes sir, I did. I was sitting at the end of the bar talking to Wizard and it was like all the air got sucked out all of a sudden. I looked up and there you were, standing in the door. I couldn't breathe. So I ran."

Her knuckles brushed across my skin as she peeled my shirt off one-handed. "I...it's like I knew you. That night, in the back room. You were holding me and I *knew* you would keep me safe. How can that be, Hollywood?"

This was the opening. I should tell her. I started to. "Maybe some people are supposed to see each other like that. They notice each other and there's that spark of recognition. Of knowing."

"Did you feel it?" Her eyes wouldn't meet mine. I tipped her chin up, kissed the point of it then the tip of her nose, waited until her gaze was steady.

"Yeah, Lainey. I felt it. I knew the moment I saw you that you were meant to be mine."

"This is happening too fast. I should worry about why that is, but I don't care." She rubbed her hand up my chest then locked her fingers around the nape of my neck. She fell back on the bed, bringing me up to land on top of her trembling body. "I don't care," she repeated and crushed her lips to mine.

LAINEY

I WAS THE WORLD'S biggest idiot. But I didn't care. I only knew I wanted to continue feeling this way, to have this sizzling flood of anticipation swamping my system.

"God, baby." Hollywood groaned in my ear,

his erection grinding into my pelvis.

I was in shock, as I opened my eyes to meet the intensity of his gaze. I felt…powerful. I had this man's complete attention and desire. I'd never felt this way in my life. I wanted to be…I didn't know what I wanted. Reckless. Yes. That's what I wanted. For once in my life, I wanted to be reckless and take exactly what I wanted. I wanted pleasure and passion and ecstasy and all the things I had denied myself as I tried to be the good one, the responsible one.

No more. Tonight was mine. Life had ground me down and now, when I should be in so much pain, I didn't feel a thing. Yet, I felt everything.

Hollywood was an outlaw. Wild. Free. He would never be tamed. Never be mine. I understood that. And I didn't care. I wanted— needed this moment in time. I was going to grab on with both hands…okay, with one hand and four other fingers that I couldn't really grip with. But this was my chance and injured or not I was taking it.

"I don't want to hurt you." The words grated out, intruding on my thoughts. I traced his jaw which was clinched so tight I could almost hear his teeth grind together.

Then he spun away and I cried out. He moved so fast I lost what little breath I had left. A blink later, I was laying against the pillows, watching him kick off his boots and rip out of his jeans. Then he was back, his weight warm and heavy against me. I arched toward him, hooking my one good arm around his neck.

"Easy, darlin'." He murmured the endearment as he grabbed a pillow and eased it under my cast. Assured my arm was safe, he braced on his elbows, watching me.

I waited. I didn't know what else to do. He was so large, so…in charge.

"We should talk." His voice resembled a growl and his burnt umber eyes darkened. "I should be gentle and give you sweet words. That's what you deserve."

I whimpered. I didn't want those things. I wanted hard and fast and him buried deep inside me.

"But I can't. Not this time." He dropped back to me, his skin rubbing against mine. He nuzzled his lips against my neck then sucked, like he was feeding from me. He traced the curve of my shoulder with his tongue, his hands touching me everywhere, arousing me. I moaned when his hand slid between our bodies. I pressed against it, rocked my hips. I was wet, needy. A scalding wave of pleasure burned through me as he pushed a finger inside my vagina.

"Your pussy," he snarled. "So fucking hot and wet for me."

He pressed his hips deeper between my thighs, spread me wide with a hand behind my knee and then the rounded crown of his cock was pushing into me. I think I screamed. I wanted to. It felt so incredible I could do nothing but breathe though the sensation. I shuddered and he stopped.

"No," I complained. "More."

He laughed, pushed in deeper. Slow. So freaking slow. He was torturing me. I looked up. Sweat beaded on his forehead. He was torturing himself too.

"In me," I ordered. "Now." I grabbed his butt cheek and sank my nails in.

He rammed into me and I couldn't breathe again. I'd never been so full. My inner muscles were stretched to capacity, burning from it, but I didn't care. I. Didn't. Care. I rolled my hips, tried to curl away so I could arch back.

"Be still," he ordered, griping my hips with both hands to make sure I did as told. "Hungry pussy." He laughed. "Greedy pussy."

His blunt words should have embarrassed me but they didn't. Then he moved. Ohmygod, did he move.

"Do things to me." Was that me begging? "Do everything to me." Oh yeah. That was me. I was lost in a raging flood of needs and greed, drowning in him. He moved over me, surrounding me with everything that was male. He was rough, as though I'd driven him beyond control, and I reveled in it.

My lungs screamed for air and I panted, trying to get enough. My heart thundered so hard my chest hurt, and I was so hot I thought my skin might truly combust. Deep inside, my bones felt like they were melting. This feeling, him pounding into me, my desire quickening past the point of sanity...God, this was...*he* was glorious.

His hands were so strong, his mouth ravenous as it moved over me, nipping, biting, kissing away the sting when the bite was too sharp. He'd taken me over, mind and body. But it was me, now, *me* who wanted—no, demanded it all. I wanted it now. All of it. All of him. I arched up, ground myself against him as he plunged in as deep as he could go. My vision blurred but there were rainbows and flashes of lights, like a prism catching the sun. Everything stopped. It was a moment of clarity—pure and stunning in the magnitude of feelings hovering there just beyond my reach.

"Now, baby. You're mine."

I saw him, suspended there above me, the planes and hollows of his face, the shadow of the stubble he never seemed to shave, and his eyes, wild eyes, focused on me. Something glinted in them, something feral like glimpsing a wolf under the light of a full moon, then everything went nuclear and I shattered.

HOLLYWOOD

I FELT HER climax in my bones when I claimed her. *Ours*, my wolf chimed in. He wanted to shift, to feel her fingers in his fur, to lick her face and sniff her, roll in her scent. When I saw awareness return to her eyes, I pumped into her again and again. Her shining blue eyes went smoky, going opaque an instant before I buried my dick balls deep in her greedy pussy and my face in her hair as I emptied into her.

Her body was drenched and felt boneless beneath me. She was trapped under my body, her breathing ragged. Or mine was. I was so damn proud of the dreamy, sated look I'd put on her face, of her breathless whimpers. There was so fuckin' much satisfaction in knowing I'd done that.

"You okay down there?"

She huffed out a deep sigh that pushed her tits tighter against my chest. "I'm not sure. I think I might have died and been resurrected. How 'bout you? Everything okay up there?"

"I may have died with you, but I'm feeling okay about that." I brushed my lips across her forehead. "Lainey."

Her eyes drifted closed, but she was still smiling. "Hollywood."

"We have to talk."

FOURTEEN

LAINEY

I HELD MY BREATH. *We have to talk.* A girl *never* wanted to hear those words, but right after the most mind-blowing sex she's ever had? Worst possible time. All those wonderful endorphins fled, leaving me wrung out, on the verge of emotional overload and the compulsory tears that accompanied said breakdown threatening to engulf me.

My right arm throbbed, reminding me that it was still attached, and I hadn't had my requisite dose of pain pills.

"Dammit, babe." Hollywood growled at me as he rolled off and his feet hit the floor. "Why didn't you tell me you were hurting?"

I stared at him and something snapped inside me—like my good sense. "Because I wasn't until you jerked me out of a perfectly wonderful post-coital haze."

Did he look chagrined? I tried to keep my focus on his face, but he was standing there beside the bed in all his glorious nakedness. Holy Adonis but he was— My mouth dried up and my brain sort of stuttered before it ground to a halt.

Still speechless, I lay limp while he maneuvered me under the covers and plumped pillows behind my back and shoulders, taking careful pains—pun intended—to keep my cast steady while he propped more pillows under it. Then he went and ruined it all by pulling on his jeans. That was probably for the best. He was too beautiful to look at. I worked up a little saliva and swallowed.

He shoved his hands in his front pockets, pulling those jeans dangerously low on his hips. I went spitless a second time when I realized he hadn't buttoned up all the way.

"Can I get you anything?"

My thoughts whirled with images of him on top of me again. Of his head buried between my legs, of my mouth on hi— What the...? I looked up at him and he was blushing. Honest-to-God blushing. Big tough biker boy was turning as red as a stoplight. Why?

"You're in pain," he murmured then headed toward the living room. He returned in a few minutes with a chilled bottle of water, one of those paper envelopes the doctor sends home with a few pills inside, and his jeans buttoned and belt buckled.

"Here."

I cupped my palm and he shook two pills out, then twisted the top off the bottle and handed it to me after I tossed the painkillers into my mouth. I drank and swallowed, realized how parched I was and kept drinking.

His eyes were glued to my throat, watching me. Wow. How could that be a turn on? I had no clue but it was, as evidenced by the bulge in his pants. Which in turn, turned me on. When I killed the bottle, I set it on the bedside table and looked up at him.

"So...we have to talk?"

"Yeah."

He looked so uncomfortable standing there, all but digging a big toe into the carpet. I figured he was going to tell me he was married or something. Might was well get it over with. I patted the bed. "Sit down, Hollywood. I'm getting a crick in my neck looking up at you."

Sitting on the foot of the bed, he curled one knee up but kept the other foot on the floor. "So...there are some things you should know."

"You're married." I blurted it out, like ripping off a Band-Aid.

He laughed, and combed his fingers through his shaggy hair. I wanted to do that— bury my fingers in his hair. "Yeah, I wish it was that simple."

"Oh crud. You're already a bigamist?" I was only sort of teasing. What did I know of motorcycle club culture?

"No, babe. Not...married."

I didn't like the way he paused before he said the word "married."

"Yet."

Breathing around the tightness in my chest took real effort. "Yet?" My voice squeaked a little.

He huffed out a breath and his hand snuck under the edge of the comforter to wrap around my calf. He seemed oblivious to his action so I didn't point it out to him.

"I need to tell you some things. About me. About…us."

"Is there an *us*?" I pressed my lips together. Why did I keep blurting this stuff out and interrupting him?

"Yeah, Lainey. There most definitely is an *us*."

I inhaled. Okay. That was good, right?

"There will always be an us. You're *mine*." He studied my face and I pretended I was playing poker—not that it would really help. "I'm a Wolf, Lainey."

My eyebrows pulled together despite my best efforts. So much for hitting the casino. Not that I would. Dealing with my mother's addiction was more than enough hassle. Still, something about the way he said the word "wolf" made it seem important. Like it should be capitalized or in quotes.

"Okay?"

"The technical term is *Lupi versi pellis*. I carry an extra gene."

My brain got back on that hamster wheel. "Ohh-kay…"

"You're my mate, Lainey."

I felt the skin stretch around my eyes as they widened. And I forgot to breathe again.

"Wolves mate for life."

I sucked in air and choked. Sputtering

around the clog in my throat, I managed to ask, "What does all that mean?"

His fingers tightened on my calf and trembled. What the heck? Was he nervous? Scared? Hollywood scared? That terrified me.

"I carry a gene that makes it possible for me to shape shift. Into a wolf."

He was crazy. I was alone with a crazy outlaw biker who thought he could turn into a wolf.

"No, darlin'," he whispered, his voice breaking. "I'm a crazy outlaw biker who *knows* I turn into a wolf."

How did he know what I was thinking? I was still wrapping my head around that as he stood up, stripped off his jeans and…oh holy shit! His body contorted, did weird painful-looking things, and then I was staring at a wolf. A huge, dark brown wolf with golden-tipped fur. And his eyes—his big sad eyes—were burnt umber.

I screamed.

FIFTEEN

HOLLYWOOD

LAINEY'S SCREAM HURT my ears and eviscerated my heart. She'd jerked as far away from me as she could get, scrambling back against the headboard, clutching the bedspread—and her knees—to her chest. The scent of ammonia burned my nose as fear rolled off her in waves.

My front door slammed open and two sets of pounding feet raced to the bedroom door. A third set—lighter, daintier but just as determined followed.

Easy and Sandhog slid to a stop. A moment later, Sam shoved her way between them. She assessed the situation in a heartbeat.

"Well, damn. This didn't go well." She turned to push the two men out of the room, which was probably smart. I was barely hanging onto control in my wolf form. The animal damn sure didn't like males anywhere near our naked mate.

"Don't close—" Easy started then Sam slammed the door in his face.

Sam dropped the backpack she'd been

holding on the floor at her feet. "Well, Hollywood. You really stepped on your poncho this time, dude."

I growled, even though she was right.

"Yeah, yeah, you'll huff and you'll puff." She rolled her eyes then promptly ignored me. "You would be Lainey. Hi. I'm Sam Cross, Easy's mate. Old lady. Wife. Take your pick." Sam laughed at the confusion and horror warring on Lainey's face. "I'll back up. You know what an old lady is right? In MC terms?"

Lainey shook her head, her eyes darting between me and Sam. Shit. She looked like she was ready to jump out the window to get away.

"Okay. MC 101. There are the—" Sam cleared her throat. "*Women* who hang around the clubhouse hoping to get…laid. By any of the members. Next up the ladder are the girlfriends. They're sort of official but they come and go. Then there are old ladies. We're property of a specific member. In my case, Easy." She turned around to show off her colors. Her leather jacket had a top rocker that said "Property of," with our wolf symbol patch in the middle, underlined by the patch with Easy's name on it. "Nobody messes with me. Following so far?"

If I hadn't been watching closely, I would have missed the slight jerk of Lainey's chin in the affirmative.

"Good. Now, you can be an old lady without being a wife. Or a mate. Some of the brothers put a ring on their old ladies, making everything legal and official and stuff. Not all of them do and I've heard that sometimes, a member and his old lady will split up. They just go their separate ways, no harm, no foul. If they're married, that's not so easy to do. Yeah?" She flashed an encouraging smile. "Now comes the trippy part. Some of the Nightriders are Wolves." She cut her eyes to me. "Since Hollywood is wearing his wolf form at the moment, I'm guessing he explained about that whole DNA thing?"

Another quick jerk of Lainey's chin.

"Well, you know what they say about Wolves, right? They mate for life. When a Wolf meets his mate, he gets all…weird."

I growled again and Sam shushed me. "Don't make me get a newspaper, Wood."

That startled a laugh out of Lainey. Progress.

"Yes, dealing with a moonstruck Wolf emotionally is like potty-training a toddler in the terrible twos. Adapting physically is a whole 'nother story. These guys take sex to a whole new level."

I curled my lip at Sam's description, though she was pretty close. A moonstruck Wolf was selfish, territorial, cranky, and demanding. And we had a tendency to mark our territory. And we wanted sex with our mates. A lot of it and often. The scent of burnt toast cut through the ammonia. Good. I could handle Lainey's anger better than her fear. Another aroma brushed across my nose. Almonds and coffee, tinged with a hint of musk. I breathed a little easier. We'd get through this.

"Um...Sam? Right?" Lainey cut her eyes to me. "Can we...um...can we talk alone?"

Sam tucked her chin to stare down at me. "That's your cue, Wood. Drag your pants and your ass out of here. Change back. Get a beer. I've got your girl."

I *whrffled*, undecided. Newly mated as we were, my emotions were pinging around as much as Lainey's. Well, Lainey's were and I was getting the spillover.

Lainey? I thought her name, projected it to her.

Her eyes widened and the ammonia stink got worse. *I'll be right outside.* I grabbed my jeans in my teeth and padded to the door Sam held open for me. I turned to look at Lainey. She hadn't relaxed. *No matter what, I love you.*

I padded through the door and Sam shut it behind me. In the living room, I shifted back to human and pulled on my jeans. Sandhog had disappeared back to his guard post outside.

Easy handed me a beer. "Yeah, that didn't go well."

"No shit, Sherlock. What was your first clue?"

"Oh, the screaming, the cowering wolf—"

"I was not cowering." I growled and tilted my head toward the bedroom, trying to listen to the conversation. Sam had moved away from the door and was keeping her voice low. Bitch. But she was trying to fix my fuck up so

I should be nice. Still, I needed to hear what they were saying. I killed the beer and headed to the fridge for a second. Then a third. I'd started my fourth before Sam opened the door and crooked her finger at Easy.

Sam pressed her lips to his ear, spoke to him. Probably half their conversation was mind to mind, as mates did. I damn sure didn't like the expression on Easy's face. Sam planted a quick kiss on her mate, ducked back into my bedroom and shut the door.

Easy's eyes were troubled. Fuck. "What?"

"She wants to go home. To her mother's."

My heart twisted and my wolf whined. I swallowed around a big ol' lump of anger and hurt. Could I really blame her? "Okay. I'll take her."

He was already shaking his head in the negative. "Sorry, bro, but no. She doesn't want to see you. Sam and I will take her, swing by our house, pick up Levi and Louie. Take them home too."

"No."

"Dammit, Hollywood. You know the rules."

"Fuck the rules."

"Don't do this, man." Easy griped my shoulder and I was reminded—forcibly—why he was Gravedigger's first choice as a backup enforcer. "Give her time, Wood. She needs to process everything that's happened. Sam will help her work through it."

Sam. Yeah, if anyone knew how craptastic our life could be, it was her. She'd lost her twin sister, been kidnapped, tortured, and dealing with a moonstruck Easy. Fun times. Not.

"What about—"

He cut me off. "We've got her security, Wood." Yeah, another reason he was an enforcer. "We'll keep her safe. You need to back off. Give her time."

I crossed my arms over my chest, scowling at him. "Is that what you did? With Sam?"

"No. And I almost lost her."

SIXTEEN

LAINEY

I SHOULD HAVE left the Twin Terrors with Sam. The milk in the refrigerator was spoiled. There wasn't enough cereal in the box for one bowl, much less two, and the boys were pouting. *Sam cooks. Jonah has a Playstation. Easy plays with us.* Yada yada. My arm hurt. My heart hurt. And I was out of a job. Any job. I'd gotten cocky and quit my other two jobs. Of course, I couldn't waitress with my arm in a cast anyway so no crawling back to the restaurant to beg.

Crying or screaming both seemed like good ideas, but with Levi and Louie sitting there staring at me and Mom asleep in her room, I couldn't unleash either.

"Look, I'll take you to school today and we'll stop at Micky-D's for breakfast. Okay?" I could take five dollars and splurge on that. The goons weren't due for a couple of days and I had enough money for that payment, plus I could pay the utility bills for this month.

The back door banged open and Larry, my oldest brother, strolled in like he had every right to be standing in the kitchen. I'd thrown him out two months ago when he left his drug stuff lying around and Levi found his meth pipe and a baggie full of that crud.

"Get out, Larry."

"Aww, now don't be mean, little sister." He stalked toward me and I grabbed a butcher knife, brandishing it in his direction.

"I'm warning you. Go away." I cut my eyes to the twins. They both looked terrified. "Boys, go call nine-one-one."

My mistake was taking my eyes off Larry. When he was high, he was mean as a snake and just as quick. He grabbed my arm just above the wrist and twisted. I dropped the knife as my hand went numb.

"Now, now, sis. Is that any way to treat your big brother?" He leered at me then lowered his head to look me in the eye.

I almost passed out from the stench of his breath. His eyes were bloodshot and his skin drawn and tight. He'd lost a lot of weight but he still had a wiry strength that held me motionless.

"You're hurting me—"

The next thing I knew, I had scratch marks across the back of my hand and Larry was flying out the door. The twins sat motionless, mouths gaping open.

"You okay, babe?"

I nodded, unable to find my voice. Wizard walked over, glanced at my hand and said, "Soap and hot water, antibiotic ointment. Now.

I'll go take care of that asshole."

My little brothers giggled so I scowled at them but went to the sink to do as Wizard said. I had no clue why he was there, but I was totally grateful. He was gone about five minutes and when he walked in, he ruffled the twins' hair and winked at me.

"Took the trash out, babe. He won't be bothering you again."

I blinked, not quite sure what Wizard meant by that. He grinned, as if reading my mind.

"He knows if he shows up here again or tries to contact you, he'll disappear."

The twins did a high five and I didn't have the energy to chastise them. I was more concerned about Wizard's appearance in my kitchen. "Why are you here, Wiz?"

"I came to pick you up for work. You really shouldn't be driving that piece of shit car of yours."

"Hey! It runs. It's dependable. It might be old but I love my car."

He rolled his eyes and gave me face. Then he nudged the boys. "We're leaving in five. Ready or not." They scrambled away to finish dressing and grab their books. Thank goodness there was a cafeteria at their school. I had nothing in the house to fix for them for lunch. "You too, Blondie."

"I can't work, Wizard. Cast. Pole. They don't mix."

"Not dancin', babe."

Wait. What? Not dancing? "Doing what then?"

"Bookkeeping. You said you were studying accounting, right?"

I nodded, looking askance at him.

"Hoss sucks at the paperwork. You're gonna do the books at Chasin' Tail. Five K a month."

That was all well and good—I could at least keep the lights on and food in the fridge but it didn't touch the five thousand dollars a week I had to pay.

"I...Wiz...Look..."

"No, you look. You're Nightrider property now."

I recalled my conversation with Sam. "No, I'm not. I don't belong to Hollywood." Heat suffused my cheeks and I realized I'd balled up my left hand.

"True. You ain't Hollywood's old lady, but that don't mean you don't belong to us. You do. And we take care of our own, Lainey. You need to figure that out."

I had. They were paying off my medical bills—like $40,000 worth of medical bills. I was an excellent bookkeeper, but I darn sure wasn't worth $20,000 a month, nor would I have the nerve to ask for that much. A tear slipped out despite my best effort and the next thing I knew, Wizard had wrapped me up in his arms. I rested my head against his chest and breathed through my panic. He smelled of cherry pipe tobacco and bay rum—an old-fashioned scent that was oddly comforting. Like his hug. But he wasn't Hollywood.

My heart stuttered and Wizard must have felt it because he loosened the hug and stepped back. "You're in trouble, babe."

"More than you know," I muttered.

"And I'm not strictly talkin' about Hollywood."

I hoped I didn't look as miserable as I felt. "I'm dealing with it, Wizard."

"Uh huh."

The boys came rushing back in, tumbling over themselves like eager puppies.

"Shut the hell up out there!"

Oh, joy. Mom was awake. Time to get a move on.

🐾 🐾 🐾 🐾

HOLLYWOOD

I WAS READY to kill someone. Rip their fucking head off their shoulders and piss down the hole. That first evening without Lainey, I gave up and shifted into my wolf. I was a block from her house when I did it. The prospects on guard duty almost shit their pants. We had a long talk. The Hell Dogs had Wolves too and if they were involved in any of this, Lainey's guards needed to be…well…on fucking *guard*.

I'd met her little brothers, in wolf form, and played fetch with them. Then I realized they might spill the beans about the stray dog. Shit.

I wasn't thinking, much less thinking straight. I'd made love to Lainey, claimed her. She was *mine* and I was losing what was left of my mind because I couldn't touch her, talk to her, fuck her until we were both blind.

Now, not even a week had passed since she kicked me out of my own apartment. Since she left me. I was so fucked up, I was currently sitting in the Russian's office at the clubhouse wondering if I could take his head. Kicked back in my chair, my booted feet propped on the front of his desk, I was picturing all sorts of murder. When the Russian walked in behind me, I didn't move.

"Stop stepping on your dick, asshole."

I glanced over my shoulder, but I already knew Gravedigger and Easy were following Russki. I offered Digger my middle finger. He and Easy dragged chairs up as the Russian settled into his own chair behind the desk.

"We have a problem."

Fuck. I continued watching Russki through half-lowered eyelids. "So we fix it."

"No. You will fix it."

Double fuck. That meant Lainey was involved.

🐾 🐾 🐾 🐾

AN HOUR LATER, I sat astride my bike in the back parking lot of Chasin' Tail. Lainey was inside. I could all but smell almonds and coffee. I couldn't put this off. The information Digger and Easy shared was hard to swallow. Still...

Lainey might be my mate, but the Nightriders came first. Always. I had to confront her. My nostrils flared. Curse or blessing, being able to scent emotions made it gawddamned hard to fuck us over.

Inside, I didn't bother knocking on the office door. I walked straight in. Lainey had her back to the door, working one-handed on the computer. She had some sort of spreadsheet thing up on the monitor.

"Just a sec, Hoss. I need to—"

"Why were you doing a private dance?" I didn't give her a chance to finish what she was saying. I had to get to the bottom of the situation. Her life—and mine—depended on her answers.

She swiveled the desk chair, faced me with wide eyes and an oh-shit expression. I almost sneezed as a parade of scents hit my nose. Ammonia. Burnt toast. Pepper sauce. Bleu cheese. And finally, damp, moldy earth mixed with pink grapefruit. Shit. I'd scared her and that pissed her off. She was determined to stand up to me, but nervous. After seeing my face she was resigned to dealing with me, but it was that sweet, tart citrus scent that gave me hope. She was yearning for...something. I could only hope it was me.

Lainey straightened her shoulders and glowered. "What are you doing here? I was told you'd stay away from me."

"Doesn't work that way, babe. Answer my

question."

"Why?"

"Because it's important. Why were you doing a private dance? Hoss says you'd never done one. Ever. Why did you dance for Lug Nut?"

"Um..."

Damn but she looked cute with her nose and mouth all scrunched up and little furrows in her forehead. Her scent shifted to bleach and blueberries. She was as confused as her expression indicated. "Babe? Why did you suddenly decide to do a private lap dance for one of the Nightriders?"

"Oh. MJ."

"MJ?"

"Yes. Mary Jane. Or...what's her stage name? Girly Temple."

"The redhead?" The Russian was suddenly leaning against the door jamb. Shit. I hadn't sensed him. I really was fucked up where Lainey was concerned.

"Yes. She caught me in the dressing room that night. Her boyfriend had come early to pick her up, and she had a private dance scheduled. I wasn't going to do it, but she explained her client was one of the Nightriders and knew all the rules. She said he wouldn't touch me and that I'd get five hundred dollars plus, since I was doing her such a big favor, she wouldn't even ask for a cut."

Russki leaned closer and stared at her as if he could read her mind. My wolf was good and played nice because...Alpha. "If you have never done a private, why would you suddenly change your mind, especially that night?"

"Oh. Um." Lainey's gaze flicked to me and she blushed a little before she broke eye contact. "I...uh...I sorta need the money."

"What the hell, Lainey?"

She gulped and I caught a whiff of rotten eggs mixed with gin. She was feeling guilty about something but indignant we were confronting her. I wanted to yell at her. Shake her until her teeth rattled. I wanted to fuckin' slam my mouth against hers and kiss her until she had no breath left for words. I did none of those things. I stood there, staring at her, nostrils flaring at the stink she gave off.

I stalked toward her and she scrambled backwards, pushing the desk chair with her feet. The cast on her arm made her movements awkward as she held it up to fend me off when I caged her in by putting my hands on the arms of the chair. Her eyes—big and round and looking as dark as midnight—pleaded with me. For understanding. I couldn't give it because I didn't. I didn't understand a gawddamned thing about this. Any of it.

"Have you ever asked anyone to dance?"

I stared at her mouth, tried to decipher the words she spoke. "What the hell?"

"In the back rooms, Hollywood. Have you ever asked for a lap dance?"

"Hell no, babe. I don't pay for that shit." I didn't. Women came to me. Came on me. For me. All of them but her, and she was the only one that fucking mattered. I breathed through my mouth, trying to hide from the scents she put off. "You better fucking talk to me, Lainey. Right fucking now."

"Or else?"

"I can't save you from the gawddamned *or else* if you don't."

"Mom." Lainey huffed out a shuddering breath. "She…gambles. A lot. She owes money. I have to pay it back. Or else."

And that explained everything. Almost. Now I understood. I knew what to do. Damn fucking relief washed through me. "I need to know it all."

SEVENTEEN

HOLLYWOOD

I SHOULD HAVE taken Lainey home but she wasn't safe there. Sam and Easy were back on twin duty, and even though Lainey was pissy about being with me, she was still my mate. My wolf would go apeshit if any other Wolf got close to her right now. She refused to go to my apartment. I wasn't ready to let her out of my sight, but bringing her to Outlaws was definitely one of my dumber ideas. I held the door open for her and urged her in with a hand on the small of her back. My fingers tingled. They fucking tingled. And my dick wanted to rip through the buttons on my fly.

She stopped to get her bearings. After looking around, she glanced at me and said, "Experiencing new cultures can be weird."

I stared at her. I know my lips were twitching because I wanted to laugh out loud but I also knew she'd get pissed at me if I did. I managed to choke out, "Ah, babe? This is a biker bar. We aren't exactly a culture."

"Yes, you are. A totally alien culture. And besides, I've never been to a biker bar."

My laugh burst out before I could consider the consequences. "Lainey, you *danced* in a biker bar."

I saw the moment she realized the truth and I watched her deflate. That pissed both me and the wolf off. Then her eyes narrowed and her mouth flattened into a stubborn line. "That was different, Hollywood."

She pursed her lips, still gazing around the room instead of looking at me. Her pulse ticked up when she realized several of the guys were staring at her.

Folding my arms across my chest, I waited. When it came to talking, she wasn't the most patient one in the room. Two of my brothers came through the door at our back. Lainey squeaked and jumped toward me as they pushed past her. I caught her as she bumped into me and slung an arm over her shoulders. I liked touching her. A lot. And I damn sure liked knowing the men in this room understood that she was mine. Even if she was fighting me on that fact.

She ducked out from under my arm. My wolf and I both growled but I stifled it. Lainey faced me. If her right arm hadn't been in a cast and sling, her fist would have been on her hip in a mirror image of her left. Her expression was so earnest I wanted to kiss her nose.

"When I was dancing at Chasin' Tail, I was on a stage. There's a...a...well..." She huffed out a breath strong enough it ruffled her bangs. "It's like there's an invisible curtain between me and the audience."

"Babe, they touched you when they put money in your G-string."

"It's still different." Did she just stamp her foot? "That wasn't *me* up there. That was a persona. I was playing a role."

Something—something I wasn't even aware was there until this moment—loosened in my chest. My wolf didn't like the idea of her dancing all but naked for a room full of horny assholes. To discover she'd been playing a part was a big relief. I glanced at the cast on her arm. She wouldn't be dancing for anyone in the foreseeable future. Now she was keeping the books in the office, away from other men. Good. I would find a way to take care of her. My wolf liked that idea a hellava lot.

I steered her further into the joint toward a tall two-top that was empty. I hadn't eaten all day and I was snarly. I pulled the second barstool around so Lainey would be sitting next to me. I could touch her, watch the room, and she could watch too. Her eyes darted everywhere and I caught a hint of ripe bananas. She was a curious little thing.

Another group of guys entered, all Nightriders. One tossed me a two-fingered salute. I hadn't seen Smoke Jenner in a couple of months. The Russian had him doing circuit rides, checking in with local chapters, troubleshooting, and probably sabotaging Hell Dog compounds. Smoke came by his name honestly. He was an arsonist and bomb tech of the first order.

Smoke grabbed a beer from the bartender and sauntered over. He looked Lainey up and down and I felt her bristle beside me. Then Smoke turned his attention on me, ignoring her. "Good to see you, Wood. Came across some interesting info about an old buddy of yours."

"Yeah?"

"I left the file with the Russian. Y'all need to look into a cop named Gerald. And his partner."

And wasn't that interesting. "I'll get with Russkie."

I looked down. Lainey's left hand was squeezing my thigh. I glanced at her. Brows scrunched over her, lips pressed tight, she stared at me and I inhaled the scent of new cut grass and rain. She was concerned about me. Did my face give that much away? I cut my eyes to Smoke. He was watching Lainey and my wolf got up to pace.

"You've got a good one there," Smoke said, his voice pitched low. "Hang on to her."

"Yeah."

Lainey and I watched him head back to the bar and the group of Nightriders gathered there. I didn't know what to think about his revelation. My mom had died in a house fire. Smoke knew all about arson, would have been a hellava investigator if he'd been on the other side of the law. I needed to get to the compound, take a look at that file. Did that scumbag cop have something to do with my mother's death?

"Hollywood?"

I focused my attention on Lainey. I had to deal with her shit before I could get to my own. "What, babe?"

"Why are those two men glaring at me?"

I looked up. Gravedigger and Gunner, the Oklahoma chapter enforcer, stood in the entrance, their entire attention focused on Lainey. What the fuck? I stood up, the barstool scraping against the floor. That's the only reaction I had time for. Gunner had Lainey's arm, dragging her toward the back exit. Digger had me wrapped up, with help from Smoke, Radar, and Bull. They took me to the floor.

"Don't fight, bro," Gravedigger ordered. "I don't want to fucking hurt you."

"What the hell?"

"Russian's orders, Wood."

That only made me fight harder. Digger got his arm around my neck and squeezed. "Dammit, Wood. He's not gonna kill her. He fucking knows you mated her. But we gotta get answers. She played us. She's workin' for the Hell Dogs."

EIGHTEEN

LAINEY

HOLLYWOOD GOING DOWN beneath a pile of Nightriders was the last glimpse I had of him. The guy dragging me out was tall, dark, and silent. Plus scary. Very, *very* scary!

"Let me go." I struggled, completely ineffectively. He didn't even bother to tighten his grip on my arm. He just tugged me along, pushed me out through a door and then everything went black. He'd hooded me. I screamed, but the sound was choked off as a heavy hand clamped over my mouth.

I'd never been claustrophobic—not that I'd known but now? I kicked. I used my right arm, flailing with my cast, not caring when I connected with my attacker...or attackers. More than one voice penetrated my panic. An arm circled my waist and picked me up. I tried to kick backwards but strong hands grabbed my ankles, shackled them with fingers that felt like iron.

I knew I was crying, knew I was hyperventilating, knew I'd pass out if I didn't control myself. I was smart. I needed to calm down and focus. I forced my muscles to relax completely so that I slumped. Whoever held my feet let go and I was hoisted into a man's arms. Moments later, my kidnappers stuffed me in the backseat of a big SUV. I remained limp as someone climbed in beside me and rested a hand on my hip. I bit the insides of my cheeks to keep from tensing up. They needed to believe I was unconscious so they'd feel free to talk. Only then could I plan for my escape.

"Russki wants to question her then we'll cut her loose." A voice I didn't recognize, but belonging to the man whose hand kept me from rolling off the seat every time the driver took a corner.

"Maybe we should use her for bait. Catch us some Hell Dogs." Another strange voice, coming from the front seat.

"Pisses me off she trapped Hollywood." A third voice, also sitting in the front. I didn't understand any of the things they were talking about. I'd finally figured out that the Hell Dogs were a rival motorcycle gang and they were even worse than the Nightriders. How could I be used as bait? I had nothing to do with them. And what did that jerk mean I'd trapped Hollywood? How?

"Can't choose who our mates are." The man touching me. And he was using that m-word again. Wait! My heart started hammering and I couldn't help the gasp that followed. "Chill it. Bitch is awake."

I stiffened. My hands weren't restrained so

I reached for the hood. A hand griped my wrist and I cried out, shuddering. He wasn't really hurting me but the flashback to the night of my injury overwhelmed everything. I went into total meltdown mode.

"What the fuck?"

The hood whipped off my head and I blinked blearily, even though it was dark outside the vehicle. Tears streamed down my cheeks and my bottom lip was bloody. I could taste copper from where I'd chewed on it trying to keep quiet. I gulped in huge gasps of air. Then I was wrenched up to a sitting position a second before my head was forced between my knees.

"You two gonna enlighten me?"

One of the guys in the front cleared his throat. "Her arm. And stuff. I guess."

"PTSD maybe?" the driver added helpfully.

"Breathe," the guy next to me ordered.

The door next to me opened and the next thing I knew, the Russian was leaning in. He grabbed my chin and jerked my head around to face him.

"Why did you betray us? Betray Hollywood?"

I sniffled and really needed to wipe my nose but my hands were caught and so was my head. "I d-don't know what you're t-talking about. How d-did I betray you?"

"You are working with the Hell Dogs."

"I don't know any Hell Dogs," I wailed.

The Russian stuck his nose against my

neck and inhaled deeply. I shivered. He released me and rocked back. "Interesting," he said. "Her brothers are already in route. Take her home. We are done with them."

Done with them? I balled up my fist and pounded against the Russian's chest—his really hard chest that would probably leave bruises on the heel of my hand. "If you hurt my brothers—"

He grabbed my fist and I froze. The look on his face was utterly terrifying and I knew. I saw exactly what he was. Feral. A predator. He'd kill me without a second's regret. I couldn't breathe.

"We do not harm innocent children." He stood up, dropping my hand. "You have made your bed, Lainey Walker. Now you will live or die in it."

I blinked and he was gone, the door already closed. I choked on every breath I took. What had just happened? No one spoke as the SUV picked up speed. Twenty minutes later, we rolled to a stop in front of my house. Lights were on inside. Mom's car was in the driveway. So was mine. The Nightriders were nothing if not efficient. Bastards.

Not waiting for permission or help, I pushed open the door and clamored out. I almost tripped over the curb but hands steadied me. Tall, dark, and deadly again.

"You're on your own, girl."

I glared up at him. "So what else is new? I've always been on my own."

He studied me, unblinking. "No more Nightrider protection."

I shoved my cast in his face. "This is what Nightrider protection got me."

The front porch light flickered on and I turned my back on the man. Marching up the broken concrete to the front door was an exercise in balance. I stopped on the front step and turned back. The man still stood there, door open but no interior light shone to silhouette him. My insides turned liquid again and my lip quivered.

"T-t-tell Hollywood t-t-to eat shit and d-d-die. I'm d-done. We're done." My voice grew stronger. "I never want to see him again. He's dead to me."

🐾 🐾 🐾 🐾

NO MORE NIGHTRIDER PROTECTION.

I found out what that meant 48 hours later. A certified letter from the hospital was hand delivered. The entire amount of my emergency room, surgery, and hospitalization was now due, payable in full. $45,216.98. Let me just cash out a few CDs, maybe sell some stock, and I'd get right on paying that. At least my sarcasm gene had remained intact.

Mom's response was to dump the twins on me and head to the casino. Her debts had continued to pile up, as I discovered when two thugs kicked in the front door.

I had the phone in my hand, dialing 9-1-1,

when they walked into the living room. Levi charged one, Louie the other. Both of my brothers yelped as they were backhanded. I was screaming at the men to get out when the 9-1-1 operator connected.

"Get out! Hello? Hello?" I yelled at the phone.

"What is your emergency?"

"Two men broke in. They hit my little brothers. I think—"

"Put the phone down, bitch." I looked up to see a very large pistol pointed at me. The second guy had some sort of gun—like from a spy movie—swinging the barrel from one twin to the other.

I whispered into the phone, "They have guns. Please hurry." I dropped the receiver.

"You're behind on your payments. The boss ain't happy."

"I...I have some money. I'll give you all I have but I have to go get it. I can meet you later. Just go away. Don't hurt my brothers."

One of them looked me up and down and my skin crawled. "Boss says you can work off your old lady's debt."

"How?" The word came out as a bare whisper.

"You got tits and a cunt, a mouth and a hole in your ass. Plenty of dick that'll pay. You spread your legs and whatever else the boss wants, the debts'll stay current."

Wait. No. Not current. They'd continue to give my mother gambling money. I'd never get what she owed paid off.

"Your pussy n'ass'll keep your brother in meth and your old bitch in chips." The guy reached down and grabbed Levi. "And these two can keep breathin'."

Sirens wailed in the distance. My call must have stayed connected. Help was coming. Levi hit the floor with a thump as the thug released him. "Talk to the cops, we'll burn your fuckin' house down around your ears." Then they were gone.

By the time the police arrived, I was numb. The twins were terrified and hiding behind me. I could only shake my head at every question the officer asked.

"Mistake," I finally managed. "I shouldn't have called. I'm sorry to have troubled you."

The younger cop looked sympathetic and kept urging me to make a statement. The older one just got impatient. They left finally. I got the boys into bed. I fixed the door the best I could using a hammer, some nails, and a screwdriver. Then I grabbed Larry's old baseball bat, pulled a chair up in front of the door, sat and waited.

NINETEEN

HOLLYWOOD

I WAS ABOUT two seconds from going rogue. The Russian told me to stay away from Lainey, that if I didn't, he'd rip out my throat. Fuck. She was my mate and my wolf was ready to chew my hand off to get to her. I needed to find out what was going on. Lainey was holding out on me. Every time I'd asked for a full explanation of her situation, she danced around the subject. And the Nightriders were my family. They'd taken me in as a kid, raised me. They had my absolute loyalty.

Ours. Mate, my wolf insisted. Yeah. I was fucking screwed. I had two choices. I could stay and play nice as a loyal Nightrider or I could go rogue, claim my mate—who might have betrayed me, and get our asses as far away, as fast as we could go. I'd be on the Nightriders' Most Wanted list for the rest of my life. I was considering it.

I heard a woman crying and my heart rate tripled. Lainey. If they'd hurt her, all bets were off. I barged into the basement room beneath the clubhouse. A man was spread-eagled on the wall, blood dripping from places where his skin had been peeled off. A woman in a skimpy denim skirt and black bra was tied in a wooden chair.

Candy-red hair. Curls. *Not* Lainey. I breathed around the burning in my chest. The Russian, standing just inside the door, glanced over his shoulder. "You should not be here, Hollywood."

My lip curled up in a snarl, and I would have taken a swing at my Alpha, but he turned to face me. The regret in his expression kicked me in the gut. He pushed me out of the room and the rusted iron scent of blood clogged my nose. Russki wore a black T-shirt and while I couldn't see the bloodstains, I could smell them. His shirt was soaked. I continued to watch him, my wolf gnawing on my gut. He wanted out to claw and bite, shredding the man standing before us, Alpha or not.

Russki dropped his chin to his chest and rubbed the back of his neck in a gesture conveying regret, one that was completely out of character. "We do not choose our mates, Hollywood. If yours has truly betrayed us, I will lock you up in order to do what needs to be done. You know this, yes?"

I could only nod, my throat too constricted to speak. If Lainey had betrayed the club— betrayed me... No. I couldn't go there.

"The other dancer made the allegations. She has been at Chasin' Tail for much longer and without the suspicious circumstances. We will question her further. She maintains that she has no boyfriend, that Lainey pressured her to relinquish the appointment with Lug Nut. She says Lainey spoke often of a boyfriend, one well-connected, and that Lainey was only dancing to get information."

Arms circled my chest, clamping my arms to my sides. Good thing. I was ready to either take on the Russian or put my fist through the concrete wall.

"You need to take gate duty, Wood."

Gravedigger. I had about as much chance taking him out as I did the Russian. I jerked my chin toward the guy shackled on the wall. "Who's he?"

Easy held up a patched leather jacket. A horned dog. He indicated the hysterical woman with a tilt of his head. "She says he's Lainey's boyfriend."

Claws sliced through my fingertips and my joints started to pop. I was an instant away from changing. Digger still held me immobile and Russki grabbed my jaw, forcing me to look into his eyes.

"You will not do this." His voice had the bite of cold steel and there was no way I could disobey. "You will go with Gravedigger and do your duty to the club. If the Hell Dogs come, I need you on the gate. Do you understand?"

He read my answer in my eyes and released my face. He nodded to Digger and that fast I was free.

"You'll need a slicker. It's rainin' like a

sonavabitch out there."

I snarled and pushed past Digger. Great. I'd go stand in the fucking rain and feel sorry for myself. My fucking mate was fucking some asshole who was a Hell Dog. I'd kill her myself if the Russian didn't.

LAINEY

I HAD TO BREATHE, had to control the panic threatening to cripple me. They'd come back while I was gone. I'd left the twins home alone. Idiotidiotidiot! I knuckled tears from my eyes. I didn't have time for tears. My brothers were missing, a note left behind saying, "Time's up." They'd left instructions and it wasn't pimping me out that they wanted this time. They wanted me to go to Chasin' Tail and doctor the books. They wanted me to set up Hoss and the Nightriders.

Hollywood, all of them, had deserted me. Those thugs had written their message on the back of my hospital bill just to make their point. I should just do it. In all the crap that had gone down, Hoss had forgotten to take my keys. I'd bet they hadn't changed the locks, or deleted my alarm code. I'd started going in early in the morning, after taking the twins to school so I could work without interruption.

And now this. I was driving in the rain like a maniac. Raining? No, not just raining, it was pouring. Buckets. The windshield wipers shuddered, as if they couldn't push the water off the glass. My headlights flickered as they illuminated the river of water rushing through the low spot in the road.

Turn around, don't drown. The warning words buzzed through my brain as I stopped the car. The engine coughed and with my foot on the brake, I revved the motor. It coughed again. Died. Damn it, damn it, damn it. I slammed my hand against the steering wheel.

Here I was, stuck on a dark road on the edge of town. After midnight and not another set of headlights in sight. I wasn't even certain of where I was going. I had only a vague idea of how to find the place I was headed.

I had 24 hours to fix the books or my little brothers would be delivered to me in bits and pieces until I'd done as they wanted. I had no idea who *they* were or why they wanted so badly to take the Nightriders down. I didn't care. I just wanted my brothers back safe and sound. And I wanted away from those men. They wouldn't leave me alone once I did this. They'd keep coming back for more until I had nothing left to give them. There was only one thing I could do.

Cranking the starter, I pumped the gas pedal, praying my car would start. It whined, coughed, caught then chugged a couple of times and died. I grabbed my phone, pressed the button to wake it up. Nothing. No car. No phone. No time. No choice. I'd have to walk.

I searched through the car. No raincoat. No umbrella. Great. Looking out the window, I realized more water was flowing along the street, and it was creeping up almost to the bumper of my car. I had to get out or risk getting washed away. Pushing open the door, a gushing waterfall of rain drenched me. Stumbling, I clutched the door to stay on my feet. I had to get to high ground. I noticed flickering lights way down the intersecting street. Maybe I could find help there. Time was running out for my brothers.

Ten minutes, an hour, I couldn't tell how long I'd been trudging through the storm, but I finally reached the entrance gate. Locked. Of course it was. I yelled, tried to rattle the bars. A figure in a black slicker emerged from a gatehouse.

"My car died. The storm," I shouted. "Can I use your phone?"

The hood slid back. Hollywood. By pure dumb luck, I'd found my way to Nightriderland—and the man I never wanted to see again, but whose help I desperately needed.

"Love the wet T-shirt look, babe."

I'm sure he did. I wasn't wearing a bra, it was freaking cold and I was drenched.

"But the whole drowned rat thing? Yeah, not a good look on you." Hollywood smirked and I curled the fingers of my left hand, wanting to hit him.

"Gee, thanks," I muttered at the same time

I realized his voice was hard, and as cold as I was standing out here in the rain.

His smirk got bigger as he unlocked and opened the gate just wide enough for me to slip through. He grabbed my right arm, lifted it.

"Dammit, babe, you got your cast wet." Emotion flashed in his eyes and then was gone, his expression settling back into hard lines.

"Duh. Raining buckets and gallons out here."

He let out a piercing whistle and within moments, two guys jogged up. "On the gate," he ordered.

The two stared at me but didn't say a word as Wood hustled me toward the...what was this building? An old train station? It was built of gray granite and looked Art Deco. Wow. I headed for the wide double doors on the front, but Hollywood steered me to the right. He guided me around the side and across an open space toward a second building that resembled a dormitory. Turned out, that's what it was.

A stairway faced the door we entered while long hallways stretched off to the sides. Wood led me down the left hall, stopped at a door and unlocked it. He ushered me inside a room holding a large bed, an entertainment center with a big screen TV, and a chest of drawers—almost an exact copy of his apartment bedroom. He herded me toward a door on the far wall. "Bathroom. Hot shower. I'll call Doc to come fix your cast."

I dug in my heels. "Hot shower won't do me

any good without dry clothes. And I don't have time. I need—"

"Do as I say."

I backed up but he stalked me. "Hollywood..."

"Lainey..."

"But..."

"My territory, babe, my rules. You're the one who showed up at my door."

Technically, it was his gate where I showed up, but in my defense, I'd had no idea I was trudging through a flash flood toward the Nightriders' inner sanctum—even though I'd been looking for it. Besides, I had no desire to see him. We'd parted ways. Okay, I'd kicked him out. I couldn't afford to get involved with a badass biker like Hollywood. I couldn't afford to get involved with the Nightriders, except I couldn't afford not to. Not now.

First they took care of me, and then they threatened me and threw me to the wolves, a phrase far too literal given what I knew about Hollywood. I was on a Tilt-a-whirl spinning out of control and I couldn't get off. I'd come to find Wizard since he worked at Chasin' Tail, and I knew this was his night off. Instead, I got a pissed-off Dreamy McTall.

"Besides, I'm not here to see you." He folded his arms over that very spectacular chest and arched a brow that only made him infuriatingly handsome. "I don't have time for hot showers and your mind games."

"Towels are on the rack."

Too late, I realized he'd backed me into the bathroom. He pulled the door shut, right in my face, before I could respond. I reached to lock it, but there wasn't one. Crap. My teeth started to chatter so the moment of truth had arrived. I had to get warm, but did I trust Hollywood?

Yes. In a completely illogical and likely insane way, I did trust Hollywood. He wouldn't barge in and bother me. He wouldn't bother to seduce me. Because he knew he didn't have to. Damn him. I still had feelings for him. And maybe that's why I'd come. Maybe I wasn't here to throw myself on Wizard's mercy, but to collapse into Hollywood's arms so he could fix everything I'd so royally screwed up.

Shaking so hard now I could barely undress, I peeled out of my wet clothes and left them in a sodden heap in the sink. The water was steaming as I stepped into the shower and pulled the curtain shut. I knew time was running out, but Hollywood was right, damn him. I needed to warm up and get dry clothes before I could convince him to save my brothers. No. Not Hollywood. Wizard. Wizard was my friend. Hollywood was...I didn't know what.

🐾 🐾 🐾 🐾

HOLLYWOOD

"I DON'T KNOW what the fuck she was doing out in the storm, much less half a mile away."

Digger and Easy weren't convinced. "Did you find her car?"

Digger nodded. "Yup. She was headed this direction."

That didn't make sense. Why was she coming here? The last I heard, she'd made it abundantly clear that she wanted nothing to do with me. And the Nightriders wanted nothing to do with her. They were convinced she'd betrayed us and the Russian was a wolf's whisker away from sacrificing her. He was torturing two people right this minute not a hundred yards away—two people involved in this whole fucked-up mess.

I paced the length of the hallway and came face to face with Sam. She shot daggers at me with her look, brushed past, and marched down the hall to her husband.

"Sam?"

"She needs dry clothes, Easy. I saw her when—" She jerked her thumb over her shoulder my direction. "Mr. Asshole there dragged her in here."

"Sam—"

"Don't fucking *Sam* me, Easy Cross."

"This is club business, Sam."

"Ask me if I care. I brought dry clothes for the girl. So shoot me." She pushed past Easy, ducked into my room, and emerged a moment later, empty-handed. "I'm headed to the house. Don't bother coming home unless you want to sleep on the couch."

"It's flooding out there."

"And I have a four-wheel drive Jeep rigged to run and used to work search-and-rescue. Don't push me, Easy. I'm really pissed at you right now. At all of you. Club business my butt. She's Hollywood's mate. Allegedly. And you're all treating her like trash you can just wad up and throw away."

She left Easy standing flat-footed and flounced past me on the way out. Gravedigger and I both eyed Easy but neither of us spoke. We weren't stupid. The tension ramped up when Digger's phone pinged with a text. I started pacing again while Dig exchanged messages with someone.

Why the fuck was Lainey out in a storm, headed here? Little Miss Two-face and I were way overdue for a long talk.

TWENTY

HOLLYWOOD

LAINEY TOSSED HER left arm up in frustration. Her right remained anchored in its cast and a new sling. Doc Carson had fixed it up as best he could. We'd have to take her into his clinic for X-rays and a new cast in the morning. The burnt toast scent of her anger scorched my nose. What the fuck did she have to be angry about? I'd come with what I figured was good news. Then ammonia edged in.

"I need to go." She said it quietly, head down.

"No."

She huffed out a breath and my gaze caught on her chest, her breasts lifting and falling beneath the bulky gray sweatshirt with enough motion to make my mouth water.

"Why am I still here? I don't get it. You're done with me. So are the Nightriders."

"Doesn't work that way, babe."

Pepper sauce spiked the odor of blackened toast. Determination. Interesting.

"You don't want me here. You and the Nightriders have made my status infinitely

clear. You don't trust me. I don't trust you."
She tried to move her broken arm and winced.
"You think I betrayed you. Fine. Whatever.
You people don't owe me a damn thing and
that works both ways. I'm done. Finished. I
have to leave so I can figure out how to save
Levi and Louie."

"We're not finished with you, Lainey. Like
it or not." *I'm not finished with you.*

Tears glittered in her eyes and something
in my chest ripped open. "Doesn't matter,
Hollywood. I'm finished with you. Let. Me.
Out."

Back stiff, chin jutting, she marched
toward the door. I snagged her good arm as she
passed me. She flinched, ducked, like I was
gonna hit her. What the fuck? Before I could
ask, someone hammered on the door, yelled,
"Time's up! The Russian wants us. Now."

LAINEY

I WISHED I had an angel. Hell, I'd settle for a
devil if I had a snowball's chance of getting out
of this mess. Since I had neither, I had no
choice. Staring at Hollywood where he stood
near the door, I did my best to look defiant.

"The clock is running out. I don't have time
to stand here debating. I didn't have to come to
you."

He showed no emotion as he stared back,

watching me through eyes feral and scary as all get out. "If you hadn't, you'd be dead the moment we discovered you'd betrayed us."

"You think I don't know that?" I threw both arms up despite the sling on my right, and immediately saw stars. My cast was still mushy and it felt like the bones were jabbing each other. "Dammit, Wood, they've got my little brothers!"

"We're aware of that, Lainey."

"Then do something, okay?" I choked, had to bend over in a futile attempt to breathe around the panic and pain searing my lungs. "I'm sorry." I didn't look up. "You don't owe me anything. The Nightriders already believe I'm guilty." I stood straight, faced him. If it was just Mom or my brother, Larry? They'd made their beds. But Louie and Levi? The twins were only ten.

"Just let me go. I'll figure something out. Maybe I can get enough money to satisfy them."

"Money's not the question, babe."

"Then what is?"

"You said it yourself. Trust."

I slumped. "You don't trust me. I understand, Hollywood. I do. You have no reason to trust me. But you just think about this. I still have keys to Chasin' Tail, and the alarm code. I could have slipped into the office at first light, when no one was around. I could have downloaded this—" I dug the flash drive out of the pockets of my wet jeans. In the pile of clothes I'd found after my shower, only the sweatshirt fit. Would the moisture from being in my pocket do something to it? Maybe corrupt the information? I held my palm with the drive on it out to the men standing around me in a semi-circle.

"I have no idea what's on this. It could be a virus, or it could be a fabricated set of books. The note said I should plug it in and follow the instructions."

A man called Radar plucked the drive off my hand. He walked over to a long table with a lap top on it and started working with his back to the rest of us.

"I could have done what they said. But I didn't. I came here. With that thumb drive. To tell you. You gave me a job when I needed one. No way was I going to betray you." I laughed dryly. "You were nice to me. And I don't want to be dead." I lifted my left shoulder. "And I would be very dead, my body probably ground up for dog food or something if I had betrayed you." I was attempting a moment of levity but it fell flat.

These men were hard. Cold. Cruel. I had no doubt that they'd killed people. I'd heard the rumors about the Russian once being a member of the Russian mob. I figured from his name Gravedigger knew where all the bodies were buried. Hardass. A man called Deadhead. Wizard. Radar. And Hollywood. Who wouldn't even look at me now. He was leaning against the door looking all lazy and at ease, his feet crossed at the ankles, hands jammed in his front pockets so that his jeans rode low on his hips. Head down, eyes on the floor, like he didn't have a bloody care in the world.

No one spoke. Everything I'd said fell into a well of deep silence. Fine. No help here. But since I'd "confessed" and turned over the evidence, maybe they'd let me walk out. I'd hitchhike home, figure something out. Maybe I could tell the bad guys I'd done what they asked, get my brothers back, and run like hell for Canada. Or Timbuktu.

I swiped at my eyes, hoping to keep my frustrated tears at bay. "I can't stand by and let my little brothers get hurt. You aren't going to help me. I get that. You have no reason to. Just let me go so I—"

"Not gonna happen." Hollywood uncoiled and pushed between Wizard and Hardass.

"You have to let me go." My voice broke and the tears came. "They're just little boys. I have to do something."

"I won't let them get hurt, won't let you get hurt. I'll protect you."

God. Hollywood looked so…angry. His face was all hard lines and the red sparks in his eyes terrified me. Before I could react, he'd grabbed my arm, jerked me against him. He smelled like baking bread and mesquite. He smelled like home. Like safety. I buried my face in his chest as his arms circled around me, holding me like I was something…fragile, something special.

"I'll get them back, Lainey. I promise."

I heard growls of dissent but I didn't look up. "I'll do anything, Hollywood. Anything the club wants. Anything you want."

That got a growl from him. Someone knocked on the door. I heard it creak open, feet shuffling, whispered conversation. Hollywood tensed and it suddenly occurred to me that he was putting himself in the line of fire. These men might kill him for offering to help me. I couldn't breathe around that thought.

"Release her, Hollywood." The Russian stood right beside us.

Hollywood growled but he did as the other man said. He put space between us, a step. Then two. His hands slid from my back to grip my biceps.

The Russian stared at me and I forced myself to meet his gaze. I couldn't remember doing anything more terrifying than looking into his eyes. As I watched, the expression in them softened though his face remained hard, his jaw clenched. He dropped my gaze, cut his eyes to Hollywood.

"The Hell Dog broke."

Hollywood's hands tightened but he held the Russian's gaze. "And?"

"We have plans to make, yes?"

I didn't know who to watch—the Russian or Hollywood. It was the twitch along Hollywood's jaw that drew my attention. He was totally focused on the Russian now. If not for the convulsive clenching of his hands on my arms, I'd think he'd forgotten all about me. I held my breath.

Still staring at Hollywood, the Russian spoke. "Take her, Gravedigger."

TWENTY-ONE

HOLLYWOOD

LAINEY GASPED AND Gravedigger had to pry my fingers from her arms. She didn't cry as he walked her out and gawddammit, I couldn't do a fucking thing but stand there and watch that sonavabitch take her away. My wolf was going ape-shit and I caught the growl emanating from Russki. I leashed my animal, breathed through the anger—the gnawing need to rip and tear and spill blood.

"They have her brothers," I finally managed to say through elongating canines.

"We will find them."

Hardass glanced at the door. A moment later, Gravedigger walked back in. "Gunner has her."

That didn't make me or my wolf happy.

"You must focus, Hollywood."

Russki continued to watch me, waiting for a moment of weakness. I might not be Alpha, but I was a damn alpha wolf in my own right. I wouldn't go belly up for him or any man. I looked him straight in the eye. "So what's the plan, boss?"

Radar raised his head. "Motherfuckers." He waved us over. "Not a virus exactly. If Lainey had plugged this in, we'd have been up shit creek for damn sure. Assholes are sophisticated, I'll give them that. They've got a code monkey who is fucking good." He flashed a feral grin. "I just happen to be better."

"Explain, Radar," Russki demanded.

"They dummied a set of books. Looks just like ours. Someone was in our system—"

"It fucking wasn't Lainey."

Hardy's hand landed on my shoulder. "Back down, Wood. We know."

I breathed in through my nose and let it out in a long huff. Radar gave me a quick nod before continuing.

"I don't think they hacked in but I'll have to look at the computer in Chasin' Tail's office to be sure. I think somebody was in the office and grabbed a screen shot, and their geek worked up the spreadsheets from that. They're smart. They have what looks like a legitimate set of books and a shadow set. They added a trapdoor plus remote access software. They'd have a pipeline to our info."

He fixed his gaze on the Russian. "Chasin' Tail wasn't always legit. Since you became prez, we've cleaned it up. The books are square. Their shadow spreadsheets are cooked, made to look like we're laundering a shit load of money through the club."

"If you were to install this software, would you be able to trace it back to the source?"

Radar leaned back in his chair and scraped his fingers over his beard stubble. As keyed up as I was, the sound rubbed me raw, like keys scraping a custom paint job on a high-dollar bike.

"I'll need to do some coding of my own, Russki. We'll want to use a dummy computer."

"Why are they doing this?" Deadhead scratched his belly, his expression perplexed.

"That is the question, now isn't it?" Russki replied. He glanced around, nailing each of us with his stare. "You have your orders. Call in whoever you need."

My brothers headed for the door, some pulling out phones to send texts or to call reinforcements. A wave of nausea hit me and my heart hammered in my chest. Lainey. Something was wrong. She was hurt.

The Russian grabbed my arm. "The mating bond, yes?"

I managed a nod, figuring from his expression that I looked as bleak as I felt.

"You must hang on, Hollywood. For your brothers. And for hers."

Yeah. It was all about brotherhood and family. Even when it was only about brotherhood and family.

LAINEY

FISTS SLAMMED AGAINST the door and I

jumped. I couldn't help it. When my dad was around, it meant he was too drunk to find his keys and things were headed downhill in a hurry. I was shaking so hard I swear my bones were rattling. Sudden heat at my back and warm breath on my cheek caused me to jerk but the strong arm sliding around my waist held me still.

"Shhh, baby. You're safe. I'm here."

Safe. Wow. Now there was a concept I hadn't considered since I was five and saw my dad slug my mom the first time. Wood's body was tense, a coiled whip ready to lash out. But not at me.

"I've got this. I'll take care of you. No sound, yeah?"

I nodded, mute as he'd asked. He slipped around me and the hair on my arms prickled. The guy gave me goosebumps and this time? It wasn't in a good way. Power rolled off him. The big, black pistol in his hand hadn't been there a second before. Greased lightning. That's how he moved. There and gone, a sliding shadow sparking electricity.

He paused at the door, listening. I couldn't even hear him breathe. More thumps and the door knob jiggled.

"Open the fuckin' door, bitch. Time to pay up, one way or another. We know you didn't do what we told you to. C'mon out here and get the first piece of this kid. Whaddaya think, Morton? A hand? Or maybe his tongue."

I clapped my hand over my mouth to keep

from screaming. I knew Wood was dangerous, but could he take on those thugs outside the door? I'd seen them—far more up close and personal than I wanted. I watched shadows move in front of the window. Three, plus the thug at the door. Four goons. Heavily muscled, probably from steroids, they were monsters. Hollywood was lean. Broad shoulders, muscular arms, with strength hidden beneath his leather vest and long-sleeved black tee, but there were four of them—and they were all bigger.

He turned his head, stared at me and I caught a flash of eye gleam, like an animal's in the dark. The hair rose on the back of my neck and I shivered harder. Hollywood was something...else. Something wild. Something vicious. I needed to remember that. He wasn't just dangerous, he was deadly.

I backed up until my butt hit the wall. I crouched down, using it to brace my body because my knees didn't want to support me any longer. As I watched, Wood's shadow seemed to expand, getting taller and wider. Then he turned the deadbolt, opened the door, and stepped out.

"What the fuck, man?" One of the thugs managed to get that question out before the door slammed shut.

Snarls. Angry and focused. Screams. Terror-filled. Gunshots. Then a sound I'd never heard before—like a sticky sponge being peeled off a counter, only ten times louder and a hundred times scarier.

The door crashed open and...*something* stood there, haloed by the mercury security light in the yard. It was shaped like a man only there was no... My brain scrambled to find a reference to compare. A biology textbook. In high school. An illustration of human musculature. Stripped of skin. The thing lurched toward me, a blood-chilling moan wailing from the dark hole that should have been surrounded by lips. It blundered into the room, hands outstretched, searching.

A whimper locked in my throat. The creature stumbling through my living room was a man with no skin. My brain refused to process this horror and the tiny bit clinging to sanity wondered if this was some elaborate practical joke—a teen slasher movie prank with amazing special effects.

Oh, yeah. Extreme special effects because a creature beyond all comprehension followed the walking biology illustration through the door. Half man, half animal, all nightmare-inducing terror. If my bladder had been full, it would have emptied. This was not the wolf that once sat patiently beside Hollywood's bed begging me to pet him. This was...death.

The kitchen door crashed open. "Get on the ground. Police!"

Police? Who'd called the police? Surely none of the neighbors. They'd never called, not in all the times my parents had screaming domestics. Not when my dad beat the snot out of Mom before turning on Larry and me. Why were the police here?

I turned to the door, saw two men in uniform. Both had their guns out. The big one was pointing his gun at me. I had my hands up—well, one of them. My right was back in a sling after Doc Carter had put a new cast on my arm.

"Don't shoot!" I yelled. "I live here. Four men broke in—" I cut off what I was saying as I realized the cops were smiling in a really weird, whacked-out way.

The big one's finger tightened on the trigger and then it all happened in slow motion. I realized he was going to shoot me and started to drop to the floor. A blur appeared from my right—Hollywood. Someone yelled. I heard howls and gunshots. What seemed like a hundred. Then screams. Lots and lots of screams.

Hollywood lay on top of me and I felt something warm and wet soak my shirt. He groaned and rolled away. His chest...Oh God, his chest. It was soaked in blood. More blood pumped from a jagged hole in his throat.

"NO!" I screamed, my denial echoing. "NOnonononoNOOOO!" I...I needed to stop the bleeding but where? How? There was so much blood. I couldn't breathe, couldn't swallow. I tasted blood. I grabbed my own throat but it was fine.

Jumbled voices floated around me. "Get Doc." "Stop the bleeding." "Change." "Dying."

"Mating bond."

I couldn't stand the noise, the fear coating the back of my tongue. I hurt. Oh, God. So much pain. My throat clogged with unshed tears, trapping my voice.

Lainey.

"Hollywood?" Did I say his name out loud? I didn't know. *Hollywood?* I said his name in my mind.

I love you, baby. I'm sorry. His voice whispered in my head.

More pain squeezed my chest. I couldn't breathe.

"Losing him."

A choked whimper fought loose and it was followed by a freight train of screams. I curled up in a fetal ball, my cast protecting my head, eyes squeezed shut, screaming and screaming and screaming until I had no breath and darkness finally saved me.

TWENTY-TWO

LAINEY

I CAME AWAKE with muscles twitching, unable to breathe, and terrified. The room was dark and unfamiliar. I forced air into my lungs, but only managed shallow breaths. I heard voices nearby—probably from the next room.

"You should not have separated them."

I recognized that voice. The Russian. And boy was he angry.

"I couldn't work on him with her there." That voice was familiar too. Doc Carter? Maybe. Where was I? Who were they talking about? Then it hit me. Everything came flooding back. The men. Hollywood turning wolfman. The cops. They were going to shoot me, but Hollywood... I choked, couldn't breathe again. Hollywood jumped in front of me. Took all the bullets. So many. I remembered hearing so many shots. I held up my left hand, but could barely see the pale outline of it in the oppressive dark. I didn't see any blood though, in my imagination, I could see it and feel it—hot, viscous as Hollywood's life drained out of him.

I couldn't stop the sob that had built up in my chest and burst out with a sharp cry.

The door flew open and light flooded in. I retreated, cringing against the pillows at my back.

I didn't expect the voice or soft hands that touched me. "You're okay, Lainey. Safe. Okay?" Fingers brushed hair away from my face. "Remember me? I'm Sam."

I did remember her. Vaguely. She…was with Easy and they'd taken care of Louie and Levi. Oh, God.

"The twins?" My question was a screaming demand.

"Shhh, shhh," Sam soothed. "The club is out looking for them. The guys will find the boys and bring them home."

"No. Nonononono. This…it all went wrong. Hollywood. Where's Hollywood? He promised to keep them safe. To find them. But…oh God." I'd never cried so much in my life, but even though my eyes and throat burned, no tears came. "He's dead, isn't he?"

Sam glanced over her shoulder to the men crowded in the doorway. The Russian shook his head. "No, he lives still."

I caught the implication, the words he didn't say. *For now.*

"I have to see him."

"Yes." The Russian flicked on the lights and I blinked against the searing brightness. When I could see past the light flares, I realized I was back in the hospital only…not.

"Where am I?"

Dr. Carson appeared next to the Russian. "A patient room in my clinic. You need to stay where you are."

The Russian hit him with a stare that made me want to pee in my pants. "Take the IVs out or I will. She needs to be with him."

A few heartbeats later, the doctor did as he was told. The Russian scooped me up into his arms with a gentleness that startled me in its exquisite care. We didn't go far. There was a large mattress on the floor of the next room. The man carrying me stopped just inside the doorway.

A huge, dark brown wolf with golden-tipped fur lay in the middle of the mattress. Bandages wrapped around his throat and his chest. I could see skin where the thick fur had been shaved. An IV needle was feeding liquid into a vein in his foreleg. And his eyes—the big, sad, burnt umber eyes I was desperate to see—were closed.

"He's dying." I could feel his life ebbing away, and I wanted to grab onto the thin tendril with both hands so I could jerk him back.

"Yes," the Russian said.

I hadn't realized I'd spoken aloud.

"You can save him."

I whipped my head around to stare at him and collided with his chin. It was like banging my temple on granite. I blinked away the pain.

He looked unfazed. "I'm not a doctor."

"No. You are his mate."

I'm pretty sure I looked completely lost—like he was speaking Russian instead of English. "I don't understand."

"You are his mate. His wolf accepted the mating bond. Hollywood extended it to you." I was still confused so he continued. "You are his mate. Honor the bond. You can keep him here. He will live for you."

"How? I...this is...it's like science fiction. Or...high fantasy or something. I feel like I'm in the middle of Beauty and the Beast."

"Accept him or lose him, Lainey Walker."

"I don't know how!" My left hand curled into the Russian's T-shirt and I jerked the material before thumping his shoulder.

Sam appeared next to us. "That's the easy part—and the hardest part of all. You have to love him."

Love him? How could I love a man I didn't know? They made this mating thing sound like some chemical imbalance, like being hypoglycemic or something. I struggled against the Russian's hold. "Put me down."

He did, but kept an arm around my waist to steady me. The wolf—no, not a wolf, Hollywood—whimpered in his sleep and one foot twitched. None of this added up. Numbers had always been my forte. Juggling them, balancing them, reconciling them. There was no juggling, balancing, or reconciling what was happening here.

Something brushed across my mind, like long fur on a wagging tail. A whisper of sound. I focused inward, trying to grab that elusive touch.

Lainey?

My name. I looked around, but I was alone in the room, swaying a little on unsteady feet.

Love.

I concentrated on the wolf. His tail...did it move? Just a whisper of a wag? All my strength leaked out and I let gravity take charge. On one hand and knees, I crawled to the mattress. It was like a hospital bed, covered in a clean sheet. I didn't know where to touch the wolf, didn't know how.

"Hollywood?" My voice broke as that lifeless tail thumped the bed once.

Instinct took over. I scooted behind him, curled my body around his back and carefully stroked his side. I kissed the fur between his ears and smiled when one twitched.

"Don't leave me," I whispered in that ear. "I don't know what this is, but I know I don't want you to go. I need you, Hollywood. I want you."

A low whine, a brush of his tail against my bare legs.

Lainey.

The voice in my head was stronger. "I'm here, Hollywood. I'm here. And I'm staying."

Love.

Was he telling me he loved me or asking if I loved him?

Mine.

I laughed. The entire force of Hollywood's arrogance and personality was inherent in that word. "Yes, yours."

The wolf sighed, pressed back against me and feelings of contentment washed over my psyche. Maybe I was crazy. I didn't care. "That works both ways, Hollywood Hilton. You're mine, too."

HOLLYWOOD

SLOGGING THROUGH THE darkness was like hiking through swamp sludge. I had warmth and light at my back that kept pushing me. I inhaled deeply. Almonds and coffee. Cut grass in the rain. Sweet lavender. Lainey—and she was concerned about me. And hopeful. I wanted to kiss her then realized a couple of things at the same time. I was hooked up to a bunch of medical shit, and I was in wolf form.

Then I remembered. I'd gone to half form to deal with the four thugs. I took them out, with the help of the brothers hiding outside Lainey's house. One of them got away after the Russian had peeled the fucker's skin off. I followed the asshole back inside—just in time to see Gerald and his partner raise their pistols to shoot Lainey.

I'd reacted without thinking to protect my

mate. I winced, remembering the searing pain as the slugs tore into my body. I vaguely remembered changing to full human as I hit the floor. And I could still hear Lainey's screams before passing out.

The door creaked open and I came to full alert, relaxing when Wizard poked his head in.

"You're awake," he whispered.

I thumped my tail in acknowledgment.

"Good." He glanced at Lainey. Her front was curled up to my back and her right arm, still in a cast, draped carefully over my ribs. "Wanna shift?"

I wagged again.

He came over to the bed and knelt down on the edge of it. Without touching Lainey—a good thing because I probably would have chewed his hand off—he called to her.

"Wake up, sleepyhead."

I felt her stir behind me.

"C'mon, Lainey. You need to get up. Doc needs to check Wood here, I'm betting you're hungry and could use a shower."

"Are you saying I stink?"

Wiz laughed. "I can't tell, babe. All I smell is wet wolf."

I snarled at him, giving him teeth. Lainey jumped up and rolled away. That made me growl. I twisted my head—fuck that hurt! Yeah, shit for brains. Gunshot wound to the throat. I whimpered and Lainey was beside me in an instant, one set of fingers tunneling through my fur. Damn but that felt good.

Maybe I wouldn't change.

"Dude, you don't change, I swear Doc is gonna call a veterinarian."

Lainey giggled and something in my chest relaxed. She rubbed my ears and dropped a kiss on the top of my head. "I want real clothes and food. And I don't do well with icky stuff. Let Doc look you over. When he's done, I'll come back and sit with you, okay?"

Very okay.

Her eyes widened. "Did you just say something?"

Duh.

"You *can* talk in my head." She'd totally forgotten Wiz was squatting there about to bust a gut.

Yeah. Works both ways.

Her brow furrowed like she was concentrating hard. *Can you hear me? I just thought I imagined the whole thing.*

I snuffled her bare leg and ran my tongue over her skin. Damn but she tasted good. I told her that and got a huge boost to my ego when she blushed all the way to the roots of her hair.

"Well fuck," Wiz interrupted. "Now you're doing all the sexy shit in your heads. I'm outta here. C'mon, Lainey. He won't change as long as you're sitting here making big eyes at him."

Wiz stood and reached down a hand to help Lainey to her feet. She wavered, getting her balance.

"A little dizzy," she explained. "I do need something to eat." She blew me a kiss. "I'll be back as soon as Doc is finished."

Promise?

"I promise." Then she added the words I needed to hear, for my ears alone. *I love you.*

TWENTY-THREE

HOLLYWOOD

THE GOOD NEWS WAS, I was healing. Slowly, but I wasn't going to die. Doc was all grouchy, muttering about patching up idiots who had no self-preservation instincts.

"You won't be doing shit for at least a month."

"When can I eat?" I wanted a rare steak almost as much as I wanted to taste Lainey's pussy.

"What did I just say? Read my lips this time. You won't be doing shit for at least a month." He narrowed his eyes. "And that means no fucking."

Well…fuck.

"I did some of my best work putting your sorry ass back together. Then the Russian forced you to change because evidently your wolf metabolism heals faster. Spend a lot of time as a wolf and maybe you can have soup in three weeks."

"Soup? To hell with that. I want beef." And Lainey.

"Don't make me sedate your ass."

"Fuck you, Doc."

He turned and walked out the door, leaving a one-fingered salute in his wake. Damn but I liked the asshole. And he was a fan-fucking-tastic doctor to boot.

Lainey slipped in before the door closed. I'd been moved to a real room so I patted the side of the bed and she climbed in.

"Can I kiss you?"

"No." Her face fell. "Cuz I'm gonna kiss you, cowgirl." I caught her startled laughter in my mouth and it felt fizzy like soda water. My dick went hard and tented the sheet. That made her giggle harder. I liked this side her, of us. Fuck. We were mated. That made me all kinds of puffed up proud and shit. She went all boneless next to me and I had to remember I could neither pull her over on top of me nor roll her to her back and fuck her senseless.

We broke the kiss and she settled at my side. Yeah, I'd be spending a lot of energy shifting back and forth with my wolf. I wanted to heal fast so I could make love to my mate again. Lainey sighed, her head resting gently on my shoulder.

"What's wrong?"

She remained silent for so long, I was worried she wouldn't answer me. I inhaled deeply. A faint whiff of ammonia so something was scaring her a little. Bleach and blueberries. Confusion. Yeah, I understand that too. "Us or something else?" I prodded.

"Yes." She murmured it but brushed her

cheek against my skin as she moved her head to look at me. "I'm worried to death about Louie and Levi. There's been no word."

Fuck. I'd forgotten about her brothers. "What about your mom?"

Her nose crinkled like she was smelling roadkill. "She doesn't care, according to Wizard. She's on a marathon gambling binge. And no one has been able to find Larry, either."

I suppose it was shitty of me to hope her asshole big brother was dead in a ditch somewhere. Or a John Doe in the morgue. Would serve him right. But he was Lainey's family.

"Why did they take the twins, Hollywood?" Lainey's eyes glittered with tears shimmering over her anger. "Why not Mom or Larry? They're the ones who got me in this mess in the first place!"

Well, alrighty then. Maybe I *could* wish for Larry the Loser to be on a slab somewhere. There was a whole lot I wanted to find out about once the twins were safe. I wanted to know what Gerald was doing there and why he was trying to kill Lainey. I wanted to know who the loan sharks were, and who was setting the Nightriders up to take a fall with Chasin' Tail. And I wanted to know why a fucking Hell Dog was involved.

Three quick raps on the door had me moving to cover Lainey. I hid my wince from her as I listened and sniffed. Wiz. "Dammit, asshole." He was laughing as he ducked through the door.

"Shit, I was hoping to catch Lainey naked."

If I'd had something to throw at him, I would have. "Fuckin' asshole."

"Yes, yes I am. But I'm an asshole with good news." He turned his smile on Lainey. "We found your brothers. Easy and Digger have them and they'll be here in about forty-five minutes."

I eased around to look at her. She was blinking so hard she couldn't see. Fighting tears. I could almost feel her relief as the scent of baby powder wafted off her.

"Are they okay?"

Wiz nodded. "A few bruises, some scrapes. We caught them trying to shimmy under a chain-link fence. They'd almost escaped all on their own." He grinned. "No wonder those two get along with Jonah, who, by the way, has insisted that Levi and Louie stay with Sam and Easy while you two recuperate."

Lainey left to get ready to see her brothers. Doc came in with a nurse to help me shower and get cleaned up. I was dressed and even though I fought it, I was in a wheelchair when the kids arrived to be checked over. They were dirty, scraped up, and hungry, but more or less fine. Levi sported a black eye that he was fuckin' proud of because he'd gotten it trying to protect Louie. Louie had a split lip, gotten the same way.

I watched Lainey fuss over them, hugging them and kissing their hurts after they were treated by Doc and his nurse. I got jealous as hell. She was my mate. I was hurt. She was supposed to fuss over me, kiss my boo-boos. I caught a whisper of laugher in my mind.

Childish much?

Damn straight I am. Come kiss me.

Laughing out loud, Lainey very carefully arranged herself in my lap and kissed me, much to the amusement of her brothers.

"Ewwww."

"Yuck!"

A wave of energy rolled down the hallway. The Russian had arrived. Even Levi and Louie recognized something big and bad was headed our way. They ducked behind my wheelchair and peeked over my shoulder.

"It is good you are up and around, Hollywood. I will arrange to have all of you moved to the compound."

I didn't like his tone of voice. "Trouble?"

"Yes."

Lainey tensed but didn't say anything. She shifted out of my lap and stepped behind me. The boys leaned against her sides and she rested her left hand on my shoulder.

Something flickered in the Russian's eyes. I couldn't decide if it was envy or approval. Either way, he was acknowledging that Lainey and the twins were mine. Good.

Two hours later, the boys were shooting pool with Jonah and a couple of the provisional members under the watchful eyes of Sam and Teri, who was Sandhog's old lady. The inner cadre, including Wiz and me and Lainey were all gathered in the Russian's office.

"We got them," Radar announced. "I set up a worm in their remote access program which gave me a trapdoor too. I can see everything they do now. Found some interesting things along the way."

He glanced over at Smoke who took up the story. "Your cop was dirty, Hollywood."

"Gerald ain't my fuckin' cop."

"He'd been workin' with the Hell Dogs."

There was something Smoke wasn't saying and I remembered the hint he'd dropped in my lap at Outlaws. "What else, man?"

"I'm pretty damn sure he set the fire that killed your mother."

Lainey gasped but I couldn't breathe for minute. I figured she'd gotten drunk, passed out, and left a lit cigarette. I was mostly gone by then, living here at the compound with the Nightriders and learning how to be a Wolf. Still, the woman had done her best by me and loved me as much as she could after losing my father.

"Soon as I can get around, that motherfucker is dead." I cut my eyes to Lainey. She watched me, her eyes going dark blue. I got a jerk of her chin in acknowledgment. Good, she wasn't freaked out I was contemplating hot-blooded murder. There was nothing cold about what I wanted to do to that man. He'd tried to make a move on my mom and beat the crap out of twelve-year-old me

Dear Readers:

I have a not-so-secret love of MC books. There's just something about finding the gentle side of a really bad boy. When the world of my Moonstruck Wolves, detoured into the gritty, sometimes violent lives the Nightriders, I happily jumped on for the ride. These outlaw MC brothers thundered out of the dark into my imagination, and above the roar of their Harleys, they introduced themselves.

Hollywood flagged me down and demanded I write his story next. He pointed to Lainey and said, "MINE!" And indeed she is. Their story won't be for everyone. Hollywood belongs to an outlaw motorcycle club. His Nightrider brothers are outlaws. And their enemies, the Hell Dogs, think nothing of rape, torture, and murder. If readers are sensitive to these themes, this is not the series for them.

As an author, I'm always humbled when readers love my characters as much as I do. I live with these people during the course of their stories. They are very *real* to me and to know that they *live* in readers' imaginations leaves me gobsmacked. Thank you.

Again, thank you for visiting my worlds. The door is always open so don't be a stranger. Happy reading!

~Silver James

BOOKS

I have a favor to ask. People talking about a book is a priceless gift readers can give an author. When you like a book, please suggest it to your friends and consider leaving a review at the etailer where you bought this book or on Goodreads. If this is your first Moonstruck world book, please check out the rest of the Nightrider series and my other books, too.

Welcome to the darkest side of the Moonstruck world. Not every Wolf walks the straight and narrow like the Wolves of the 69th. Gritty, earthy, and violent, rogue Wolves run on the criminal side of society. Gun running, strip clubs, bounty hunters, the Nightriders live their lives in the outlaw 1%. There's sex, violence, and violent sex, and sometimes, a Wolf smacks up against the woman destined to turn him moonstruck...

Night Shift
(Nightriders MC #1)

Everybody knows you don't mess with a big, bad

Wolf. Well, everyone except Samantha Prescott...

He's Easy...

Elijah "Easy" Cross works the night shift for the Nightriders MC, collecting pay-offs, protection money, and "policing" their properties. "Live to ride, ride to live" takes on a whole new meaning when members of a rival MC—the Hell Dogs— shoot him and give chase with the intent to kill. Easy ends up on the front porch of a single mom hiding deadly secrets from the same people after him. When she's brutally murdered by the Hell Dogs, he feels responsible and promises to protect her two kids. Easy and his Nightrider brothers might ride on the far side of the law but hell, yeah their honor is worth dying for, and a promise is a promise.

And she's not...

Samantha "Sam" Prescott only wants two things from the Nightriders—her niece and nephew. It's bad enough her twin got involved with an outlaw motorcycle gang—and was murdered—but now Sam is desperate to extricate herself and the kids. To do that, she has to escape Easy, the sexy biker with boy-next-door dimples and killer instincts. It's that whole killer thing she must keep in mind when the moonstruck Wolf is determined to make her his mate. Her instincts scream, "RUN!" Her hormones want to get down and dirty with the man who turns her boneless with a kiss.

When Sam is kidnapped and tortured by the Hell

Dogs, Easy must decide to either keep his promise to ride through the fires of hell to find her or let her go for good, even if it kills him.

Warning: Lots of down and dirty sex, extreme violence—including against women—of the blood and guts kind, alpha MC members, and a moonstruck Wolf shifter with dimples. This is the dark side of the Moonstruck world where sex is rough, death is brutal, and laws don't mean jack.
3rd PLACE, INTERNATIONAL DIGITAL AWARDS EROTIC CATEGORY
FINALIST, NATIONAL READERS CHOICE AWARDS EROTIC ROMANCE CATEGORY

Remember the Night
(Nightriders MC #1.5)

Everybody knows you don't mess with a big, bad Wolf. Well, everyone except Gemma West…

If a Wolf plays his cards right, he might get lucky in love…
Ten years ago, Lucas "Lucky" Malone ran from charges of murder, leaving behind the girl destined to be his mate. Now he makes his own odds as president of the Oklahoma Chapter of the Nightriders.

When a girl's luck runs out…
Bad luck follows Gemma West like a black cloud. She just wants to go home but when she witnesses

a horrific car crash, she can't turn her back. Coming face-to-face with the only man she's ever loved might be the worst luck of all.

An accident brought them together, but an MC war is brewing and the last thing Lucky needs is to take a gamble on the one woman guaranteed to make him howl at the moon. How can this moonstruck Wolf walk away from her a second time?

Warning: Down and dirty sex, extreme violence of the blood and guts kind, alpha MC members, and a moonstruck Wolf looking to win it all. This is the dark side of the Moonstruck world where sex is rough, death is brutal, and laws don't mean jack.

Night Moves
(Nightriders MC #2)

Everybody knows you don't mess with a big, bad Wolf. Well, everyone except Lainey Walker...

Hooray for Hollywood...
Eric "Hollywood" Hilton is no hero, he's a Nightrider first, last, and always. There isn't anything he won't do for the club. With his looks, women are a dime a dozen until he walks into Chasin' Tail and smacks head first into that crazy thing called love.

Run, don't walk...
Lainey Walker only wants to pay off her family's debts and return to college. She almost walks away

but dancing at Chasin' Tail brings in the big bucks. The last thing she expects is to wind up in the middle of a biker showdown, much less get caught on the wrong side.

When it looks like Lainey will betray the Nightriders, Hollywood has to decide between his brothers and his mate. Can he prove her innocence in time to save her?

Warning: Lots of down and dirty sex, extreme violence of the blood and guts kind, alpha MC members, and a moonstruck Wolf with stars in his eyes. This is the dark side of the Moonstruck world where sex is rough, death is brutal, and laws don't mean jack.

Night Fire
(Nightriders MC #3)

Everybody knows you can't trust a lone Wolf. Just ask Leigh Daniels...

Where there's Smoke...
Brian "Smoke" Jenner is a Nightrider nomad, traveling the country doing dirty work for the club's national council. Sent to Dallas to find out who's framing the Nightriders by setting fires, the last woman he expects to light his is Leigh Daniels.

There's fire...
Leigh Daniels is an arson investigator. She lives for putting arsonists in prison. When she almost hits a dog on the way to a fire scene, she doesn't

expect to be rescued by a sexy biker—especially not one who sets her heart ablaze.

Despite her best intentions, there's no walking away from Smoke—until evidence mounts up of his connection to the fires. He claims he's innocent, but Leigh has her doubts. Will he catch the real culprit in time to convince her, or will he lose it all—the woman he loves and his life?

Warning: Lots of down and dirty sex, violence of the blood and guts kind, alpha MC members, and a moonstruck Wolf burning up for his mate. This is the dark side of the Moonstruck world where sex is rough, death is brutal, and laws don't mean jack.

****

In the beginning, there were the Wolves of Army Special SciOps Unit 69...

MOONSTRUCK: SECRETS
Moonstruck Genesis #3

Search...
The existence of Wolves has remained a secret for over 200 years. Now, the members of Army Special SciOps Unit 69 are about to be exposed. When a covert operation behind enemy lines goes wrong, Sergeant Major Ian McIntire must trust Major Hannah Jackson to save his men—and his heart. She's already privy most of his secrets but the one she doesn't know about the moonstruck alpha

werewolf may get them all killed. She has one chance to get them undercover and safe, but it may already be too late.

Rescue...

Ten years later, former Army sniper Michael Lightfoot's life as a forest ranger fits his need to run wild when the moon is full—until two wild wolf pups are kidnapped, along with Dr. Liz Graham, the wildlife biologist who makes him want to howl. The last thing he expects when he rescues the feisty doctor is to be moonstruck. With her life in danger, he must reveal his true self—and risk losing her—in order to save her from the shady corporation stalking the Wolves.

Secrets...

Secrets, lies, and betrayals are more personal under the full moon, but when a Wolf loves a woman, he'll take a secret to the grave to keep her safe.

Welcome back to the Moonstruck world with this full length Moonstruck novel containing new chapters and deleted scenes in addition to the first two novellas, **BLOOD MOON** and **BAD MOON.**

MOONSTRUCK: LIES
Moonstruck Genesis #2

Hunters...

Dr. Jacey Randolph just might be crazy. A rescued wolf is more than he seems and his ability to get into her head—literally—makes her doubt her sanity. When Colonel Joshua Harjo shows up on her doorstep with a wild tale that the wolf is actually Marine Captain Nathaniel Connor, Jacey must make a leap of faith—and jeopardize her heart—to get involved with the Wolf and a group of former Army SpecOps soldiers in full rescue operation mode.

Wolves...
Sean Donaldson answers an SOS from an old Army buddy and rides smack dab into the middle of a conspiracy. Murder and kidnapping are just the tip of the iceberg. Undercover, his best intentions are complicated by Annie Simmons and her son, Cody. What she doesn't know about the lies he's told can hurt her...and put Cody in danger.

Lies...
Secrets, lies, and betrayals are more personal under the full moon but when Wolves fight for their hearts, they'll risk everything to uncover the lies endangering those they love.

Welcome back to the Moonstruck world with this second full length Moonstruck novel containing new and deleted scenes and chapters never before published, in addition to the previously published novellas, **HUNTER'S MOON** and **WOLF MOON**.

*Available in digital format only –
the original Moonstruck novellas*

Blood Moon

(Moonstruck –Book 1)

Army Major Hannah Jackson knows where the skeletons are hidden at the Pentagon and now she's been tasked with keeping the secrets of Army Special Sci Ops Unit 69—the Wolves—and their secret is a doozy. That a civilian corporation wants to exploit the Wolves is a matter of pressing concern.

Sergeant Major Ian McIntire doesn't trust Hannah as far as he can throw her—and that's quite a ways considering he's an alpha werewolf. The woman is a pain in his butt and with the Blood Moon coming, the unit needs to complete their mission and get home before tempers flare. While she might know most of their secrets, the one she doesn't know about the moonstruck Wolf might just get them all killed.

When a covert operation goes wrong, Mac must trust Hannah to save his men—and his heart. Secrets, lies, and betrayals are more personal under the full moon, but when a Wolf loves a woman, he'll do whatever it takes to keep her safe.

Warning: Pursue an alpha Wolf at your own risk. Hot sex, bad words, and action of the blood and guts kind will ensue.
WINNER 2013 INTERNATIONAL DIGITAL AWARDS SHORT PARANORMAL NOVEL

Bad Moon

(Moonstruck –Book 2)

Former Army sniper Michael Lightfoot lives a simple life as a forest ranger in Wyoming. The job fits his need to run wild when the moon is full— until two special wolf pups are kidnapped, along with Dr. Liz Graham, the wildlife biologist who makes him want to howl.

The last thing Michael expects when he meets the feisty doctor is to be moonstruck, but the alpha Wolf has more on his plate than just convincing Dr. Liz to love him for who he is. She's being stalked by mercenaries who stole two wolf pups for an unknown faction. Now, with her life in danger, he must reveal his true self to save her. Reuniting with some of his old Army Special SciOps unit, Michael takes on the corporate raiders who want more than just his hide—and Liz's expertise.

Secrets, lies, and betrayals are more personal under the full moon, but when a Wolf loves a woman, he'll risk heart and soul to keep her.

Warning: When a moonstruck Wolf meets his mate, hot sex will ensue. If his mate is threatened, bad words and violence of the blood and guts variety will definitely occur.

Hunter's Moon
(Moonstruck –Book 3)

Dr. Jacey Randolph just might be crazy. A rescued wolf is more than he seems and his ability to get into her head—literally—makes her doubt her sanity. After the death of her husband in the Gulf War, she returned to the family ranch to run an animal sanctuary. Bad enough she has to fend off advances from the local sheriff, but now she's turning into some sort of Dr. Doolittle. Except she doesn't talk to animals, dammit.

When Colonel Joshua Harjo, an old friend of her husband's, shows up on her doorstep with a wild tale that the wolf is actually Marine Captain Nathaniel Connor, Jacey must make a leap of faith—and jeopardize her heart—to get involved with the wolf and a group of former Army SciOps soldiers in full rescue operation mode.

Secrets, lies, and betrayals are more personal under the full moon but when a woman loves a Wolf, he can do no wrong. And Jacey Randolph is not about to let a little thing like a band of mercenaries keep her from the Wolf she loves.

Warning: Explosions, death, and sex go hand in hand when a group of Wolves and their women fight for their existence.

Wolf Moon
(Moonstruck –Book 4)

Sean Donaldson, former combat medic and demolition expert, answers an SOS from an old Army buddy and rides smack dab into the middle of a conspiracy. Murder and kidnapping are just the tip of the iceberg. Going undercover with a biker gang seems the quickest solution but Sean's best intentions are complicated by Annie Simmons and her son, Cody.

Annie is a waitress at the Half Dollar Bar and Grill just scraping by to provide a better life for her son. She doesn't want a man in her life, especially a scary dude like "Boomer," the big biker who steals a part of her heart. What she doesn't know about the lies he's told can hurt her…and put Cody in danger.

Secrets, lies, and betrayals are more personal under the full moon but when a Wolf fights for his heart, he'll risk his life to make sure the family he loves survives.

Warning: When it's the month of the Wolf Moon, anybody who gets between a moonstruck Wolf and his mate deserves what they get. Blood, sex, and four-letter words dead ahead.

Bride's Moon
(Moonstruck –Book 5)

When the remnants of Special SciOps Unit 69, the Wolves, reunited to save a group of soldiers used as lab rats in a secret experiment, Colonel Joshua Harjo never expected to command the covert government unit again. Someone near the top wants the 69th back on active duty and Harjo is tasked with making it happen, along with keeping the men the Wolves rescued top secret.

Amy Rouse is the best "cat herder" around and

she's recruited for administrative duties with the new unit, a job with perks—Wolves and their commanding officer, Joshua Hargo, the man of her dreams. Amy didn't count on murder, mayhem, and a redheaded Deputy US Marshal to complicate her life.

Secrets, lies, and betrayals are more personal under the full moon, but when a man loves a woman, nothing will stop him from tying the knot.

Warning: The road to romance is never smooth and a runaway bride might just jinx a highly sensitive operation.

Rogue Moon
(Moonstruck –Book 6)

Rudek Tornjak is a Wolf without a pack. A man scarred by his past, he prefers it that way. While living in the shadows of the French Quarter, whispers of treachery and betrayal reach his ears—along with accusations implicating him in unthinkable acts. He comes out of hiding to confront his accusers only to discover he's under a death sentence. On the run, he encounters Isabelle Fontaine, a woman with a past of her own she'd rather keep hidden.

Family is everything to Izzy and she'll do whatever it takes to keep hers safe. Crossing paths with a shadowy corporation and a rogue Wolf puts the people she cares about in jeopardy—not to mention her own life and heart.

Secrets, lies, and betrayals are more personal under the full moon, but when a betrayed Wolf fights for his honor, no one is safe—not even the woman he loves.

Warning: Doubt a Wolf's honor and you'll get a serving of hot blood and guts to go.

Christmas Moon
(A Moonstruck Novella, #7)

The Wolves have been busy since blowing up half of Louisiana. Thanks to the government, there's a bounty on their heads so they're living off the grid. But Christmas is here and the kids want to know if Santa will find them this year. Not a problem until the phone call asking them to find and rescue a pregnant girl. On December 20th. In New Mexico. Piece of fruit cake, right?

Walking into a firefight with a drug cartel is never easy, but with Hannah's wrath and Liam's first change on the line, Mac and the Wolves face a harder choice—save the girl or save Christmas.

Secrets, lies, and betrayals are more personal under the Christmas moon, and it might just take the magic of Santa to help the Wolves save the day and make it home to their families in time. Because in the end, it's all about family.

Warning: Santa's making his list and when the Wolves go into action, they'll find out who's

naughty and who's nice.
FINALIST 2014 INTERNATIONAL DIGITAL AWARDS SHORT PARANORMAL NOVEL

Blue Moon
(Moonstruck –Book 8)

DJ Collier is a manhunter. As a Deputy US Marshal, she'll go after any fugitive, but the names in the secret file dumped on her desk must be ghosts considering the lack of information she can gather. Where better to hunt them than in the last place she encountered the elusive group of military Special Operators? She never expected to find death, destruction, and a sexy Wolf determined to make her his in the Louisiana bayous.

Antoine Fontaine has lived in the bayous all his life. Always standing on the outside of his close-knit Cajun family, he thinks he's one of a kind. He never expected to discover another like himself, much less a whole group of SpecOps Wolves who welcome him into their pack. He has no idea what it means to be moonstruck until he rescues a feisty Deputy US Marshal. Now, he'll fight to the death to keep her.

Once in a Blue Moon, a Wolf finds his mate and even if he's up to his ass in alligators, he'll keep her safe. Warning: Hot sex, explosions, and mayhem of the blood and guts kind dead ahead.
WINNER 2015 INTERNATIONAL DIGITAL AWARDS SHORT PARANORMAL NOVEL

Moon Shot
(Moonstruck –Book 9)
A Moonstruck/Hard Target Crossover Novel
Scorched earth...

The Wolves are damn tired of being hunted. They've licked their wounds and now it's time to take the fight to the enemy. They're moving on up—all the way to the hallowed halls of government. Intelligence reports indicate their enemies are getting closer—and more personal. Assassination of the Wolves and their families is on the menu and SEAL Team Atlantis has the kill order.

Unexpected allies, a new baby, and the healing of old wounds give the Wolves something to live—and fight—for. Every last one of them is ready for a Happy Ever After.

Retribution...

There are three things a Wolf holds sacred—his mate, his pups, and his pack. Threaten any one of them and you'd better be checking your six. Threaten all three? Just remember—secrets, lies, and betrayals demand payback and the Wolves are ready to hunt.

Warning: Wolves don't hold a grudge, they get even.

HARD TARGET

The HARD TARGET Team: Judge, jury, executioner...

The multinational Hard Target special operators hunt the worst of the worst, and each brings their own brand of special to the mix. Genetically enhanced Navy SEALs. Wolf shifters from the SAS and Irish Marines. An Israeli Oketz officer. And a team of former USAF pilots and pararescue jumpers whose humanity doesn't keep them out of the fight. All corralled by Mother Goose, who commands the undercover group with steel-toed combat boots and cold beer.

Double Cross
(Book 1)

Double-crossed...

Duke Reagan's mission went to hell. His SEAL teammates dead, abandoned by Command in the middle of an African warlord's territory, he's wounded, blind, and on the run with a terrified American, Coreen Prince, a doctor who was supposed to be collateral damage. Somehow, they survive, but not before they lose a bit of their hearts to each other.

Dr. Coreen Prince struggled to put her life back together after her African ordeal, but a slight detour one night in Key West offers her the chance to apologize to the man who saved her at such great cost to himself. Too bad Duke didn't recognize her.

It takes a year to restore Duke's vision, and the return of his sight comes with the opportunity to join the Hard Target team, a not-quite white hat organization doing what government coalitions can't. His first mission as the team's sniper puts a drug cartel boss in his sights, but a familiar face that's haunted Duke since Africa crowds the scope.

On special assignment in South America, Cory once again finds herself in the wrong place at the wrong time. But rescue comes from the last man she expects to see, the one man she can't forget. Will they get a second chance at love or will he just see her as another double cross…

****

From Harlequin Desire
The Red Dirt Royalty series:

Cowgirls Don't Cry
The wealthiest of enemies may seduce the ranch right out from under her!

Cassidy Morgan wasn't raised a crybaby. So when her father dies and leaves the family ranch vulnerable to takeover by an Okie gazillionaire with a grudge, she doesn't shed a tear—she fights back.

But Chance Barron, the son of said gazillionaire, is a too-sexy adversary. In fact, it isn't until Cassidy falls head over heels for the sexy cowboy-hat-wearing attorney that she even finds out he's the enemy. Now she needs a plucky plan to save her birthright. But Chance has another trick up his sleeve, putting family loyalties—and passion—to the ultimate test.

The Cowgirl's Little Secret
She's back at his ranch...with baby in tow.

When nurse Jolie Davis comes home, she knows it's only a matter of time before she runs into Cord Barron—the Barrons own this town. In fact, it was their oil business rivalry with her father that caused her break up with Cord in the first place. But no amount of family meddling can deny the fact that she had his secret son. Now, four years later, as her ex is wheeled into the ER—while she's on duty!—it's time to come clean. Because it quickly becomes clear that Cord is determined to reclaim her...

The Boss and His Cowgirl
When the billionaire boss beckons...

Ever since she left behind her cowgirl roots to work for him, Georgie Dreyfus has had a crush on her boss, US senator Clay Barron. So the sexy speechwriter is speechless when Clay comes to her rescue on the campaign trail…and they discover a mutual chemistry that will no longer be denied.

But when their relationship faces one of the biggest veto threats of all, Georgie goes home to Oklahoma to regroup. Now the billionaire Barron must choose: continue his quest to win the White House or win back the woman who's laid claim to his heart…

Convenient Cowgirl Bride
It's a marriage of convenience for this sexy tycoon!

Barron Entertainment CEO Chasen "Chase" Barron needs a wife like he needs a hangover. But when his latest escapades land him in the tabloids, he faces an ultimatum from the Barron family patriarch: pick a wife or one will be picked for him. That's when perfect stranger Savannah Wolfe shows up, out of the blue, in his bed! It's all a mix-up, but how convenient. The feisty cowgirl fits the bill for a fake wedding. Chase'll help her with her rodeo career if she plays along. But how inconvenient if he falls for Savannah for real in the process…

Redeemed by the Cowgirl
Everything he does is for family—including moving in with a woman he can't trust…

Cash Barron has always been the good son, protecting his father's billion-dollar empire. So when grifters target Barron Enterprises, Cash focuses on the femme fatale of the bunch. To keep tabs on Roxanne Rowland, he'll move her into his luxury condo. And one step closer to his bed...

But Roxie is innocent—just a pawn in her family's criminal game. Worse still, she's long had a crush on ruthless Cash. So can Roxie find the chink in his armor and redeem this hard-hearted, hard-muscled man?

Claiming the Cowgirl's Baby
The surprise heir gets a surprise heir!
As the newly revealed secret son of Oklahoma's most notorious billionaire, ranch foreman Kaden Waite could lose everything if he doesn't kowtow to his later father's terms. In a desperate moment, he turns to heiress and friend Pippa Duncan for some very private comfort. But soon Pippa has a secret of her own—she's having his baby. Kaden is determined that history not repeat itself, the child will bear his name and Pippa will be his bride. But Pippa refuses to settle for marriage without love. Is it a stalemate or the start of something truly special?

The Cowboy's Christmas Proposition
Can a country superstar and a dedicated cop strike a Christmas baby bargain?

Being a celebrity, Deacon Tate is always careful. So when a baby is left on his tour bus, he's 99 percent certain it isn't his. But he's 100 percent sure that trooper Quin Kincaid, who responds to the call, is the sexiest woman he's ever seen. He has to have her, no matter what.

But to Quin, Deacon seems too good to be true. Can she save the baby and herself from Deacon's spell—especially when he makes her an offer she can't refuse?

****

Award-winning Urban Fantasy

The Penumbra Papers
Cases from the Shadow's Edge
Penumbra: Etymology: New Latin, from Latin paene almost + umbra shadow

These "Cases from the Shadow's Edge" explore the forces of light and dark as they dance through shadows humans barely glimpsed prior to the Big Rip. Since then, all manner of preternatural magicks intermingle with humans in ways mysterious, magical and, in some cases, criminal. Much to humanity's surprise, there really are monsters under the bed and the things that go bump in the night are bigger and scarier than anyone ever imagined.

Vampires. Ghouls. Faeries. Ghosts. Werewolves. Creatures of legend and nightmares. Overnight, reality took on a whole new meaning. The world's best and brightest from every discipline—physics, theology, anthropology, chemistry, to name only a few—all tried to explain the rip in the cosmic curtain. Sade Marquis has her own theory. The monsters have been here all along, flying just under the radar of normal perception. They've been masquerading as mundanes—their term for humans. Of course, Sade knows the truth of the matter. She was raised by a master vampire and her pet "dog" shifted into a boy the night of her twelfth birthday. Sade's very good at keeping secrets. She has a lot of them.

This is where *Special Agent* Sade Marquis enters the mix. A human FBI agent with an X-Files mentality, Sade's been handpicked to fill a new slot within the Bureau—Preternatural Liaison Officer with the MAGIC Unit. The Magical Activity, Grievances, and Inhuman Crimes unit is in charge of investigations involving magicks. It's her job to deal with all the monsters, and she's very, very good at her job. That makes the magicks very, very afraid of her. As they should be...

That Ol' Black Magic
Penumbra Papers #1

Magic and mayhem in the French Quarter
Along with her FBI partner—and werewolf best friend—Caleb Jones, Sade is sent to New Orleans to investigate the murders of several high-ranking magicks. The Big Easy is neutral territory so Sade must find and arrest the culprit before war breaks out between the Realms. Things look up when the gargoyle Sentinel, Roman, a permanent fixture in Sade's childhood, arrives to keep the peace. Maybe.

The investigation is hampered by Sade's faerie nemesis, Ariel—the King's Seducer. Oh, and then there's the new dragon in town, Nikolas Constantine. Sade can't decide whether to arrest his ass or admire it.

When guilt and innocence come to play in the French Quarter, it'll take Sade's brand of crazy to sort it all out.

WINNER 2014 INTERNATIONAL DIGITAL AWARDS SHORT PARANORMAL NOVEL

Season of The Witch
Penumbra Papers #2

Sade Marquis: Her best friend turns furry. Her godfather is a master vampire. Her mother was once the mistress of Oberon, King of the Faerie Court.

When the Veil between the mortal and magical realms rips, FBI Special Agent Sade Marquis is in a unique position to head up the newly-formed MAGIC unit. She's the only human who knows exactly what goes bump in the night. When things go to hell in a handbasket and there's magic in the air, Sade is the agent FBI Director George Bailey wants in the trenches. She's savvy, snarky, and sexy but she may have met her match when she's sent to Chicago to investigate the murder of a congressional aide.

Is the vampire, Kristian St. John, guilty as sin?

Once a Templar knight, Sinjen now teaches history at the University of Chicago. He must rely on Sade to clear his name and track the real culprit.

Together, they unravel the clues to a mystery that began a thousand years before. If they don't solve the murders of six young women, the whole world—human *and* magick—will suffer the evil consequences.
FINALIST 2014 INTERNATIONAL DIGITAL AWARDS LONG PARANORMAL NOVEL

The Devil's Cut
Penumbra Papers #3

The Devil's in the details...
What do two werewolf teens missing in the New Mexico desert, a stolen pouch of Native American fetishes, and a drug lord calling himself El Diablo have in common? Undercover FBI Agent Caleb Jones would sure like to find out. The trail leads to Denver where CSI Adele McCoy is investigating the cases of two diabolically murdered men and the pouch of Native American fetishes discovered at one of the crime scenes. She doesn't believe in magic, but the whole situation gives her a creepy supernatural vibe she can't deny.

And the Devil always gets his cut...
When their cases collide, Caleb and Adele are soon running for their lives—and fighting an attraction that threatens to combust. Hot on their trail is Caleb's best friend, Special Agent Sade Marquis. She's bound and determined to find the wayward

werewolf. Death is a dialogue, love hurts, and you don't know the measure of a man—or a woman—until it's time to pay the Devil his due. In this Case from the Shadow's Edge, it might just be a werewolf and the woman he loves who pay the price.
FINALIST NATIONAL READERS CHOICE AWARDS

From Amazon's Kindle Worlds

Susan Stoker's Special Forces: Operation Alpha Kindle World:

Special Forces: Operation Alpha: SEAL Moon
(A Novella set in the Moonstruck World)

A Wolf haunted by his past...
Former Navy SEAL Riley "Speed" O'Brien left the Teams after his best friend died in his arms. After kicking around for a couple of years, the wolf shifter lands on the Gulf Trident, a drilling platform in the Gulf of Mexico. As Safety Officer, the lives of everyone on board are this Wolf shifter's responsibility—including the new OIM. Who just might be his mate.

A woman out to prove her worth...
Taylor Dagny has the right ticket punches and an almost desperate need to prove herself to her family, who owns the controlling interest in Delta-Dansk Exploration. Taking over as the Offshore Installation Manager of the Gulf Trident is her first step toward her future. One problem. Her sexy safety chief is determined to knock the chip off her

shoulder, and get her naked.

Under attack...
A mercenary force, an uninhabited tropical island, and two people fighting for their lives. Can this moonstruck Wolf save his mate and convince her to love him at the same time?

Special Forces: Operation Alpha: Rescue Moon (A Moonstruck companion novella)

His secret should have been safe...
Master Sergeant Hawkins "Hawk" Greenwood has all his tickets punched—Green Beret, Ranger, Delta Force, and working ops so secret they don't show up in his personnel file. On loan to Captain Ghost Bryson's Delta Force team as a survival instructor, Hawk receives new orders: rescue a school teacher kidnapped in Mexico. His full-blood Choctaw heritage is great for going undercover south of the border, but his secret ability to shift into a wolf makes him uniquely qualified for this assignment.

Her safety should have been assured...
Anthropologist Dana Peterson assumed she'd be safe working on a project for the Mexican Department of Antiquities with her group of prep school students—until the local drug cartel kidnaps them all. The kids have rich parents to pay their ransoms. Dana has no one. Abandoned by the State Department, her only chance for freedom comes in the form of a wolf attacking her kidnappers. When a mysterious man appears to guide her to safety, it's not desert heat she needs

to worry about, but the chemistry flaring between her and her rescuer.

Her blood is the key...
There's more at stake than meets the eye. Dana has a target on her back—placed there by a shady geneticist. It's up to Hawk to keep her safe and claim her as his mate because under the full moon, even hearts can be rescued.

Paige Tyler's Dallas Fire & Rescue Kindle World

DALLAS FIRE & RESCUE: CRASH & BURN
(A Moonstruck companion novella)

A lone Wolf on the hunt...
As a Homeland Security investigator with a unique set of gifts, it's Derek Alexander's job to track down the worst kind of prey—human traffickers. One step behind, he missed them in Kansas City, but after an unlikely informant puts him on the trail to Dallas, he might find his case come crashing down around his ears, taking his heart along with it.

A woman on the job...
Katherine 'Kit' Carson is a new Airport Rescue Fire Fighter at DFW International, but she didn't expect her first day to land her in the middle of an inferno. Between investigating a plane that exploded mid-air and encountering a hot government agent, Kit's work might send her into a fiery spiral of love and danger she was never trained to handle.

When duty and love collide, a Wolf and his mate are destined to Crash & Burn.

DALLAS FIRE & RESCUE: BLOOD & FIRE (A Moonstruck companion novella)

A Wolf shifter gone rogue...
For Rhys Kendric, banished from his pack as a teen, life as a bounty hunter is good. Women chase him, he can drink any three men under the table, and he hasn't lost a bar fight in years. Given the job of tracking bail-jumper Reece Chatham, son of the man who'd exiled him, Rhys uncovers an archaic pack practice: taking a blood bride. In a case of mistaken identity gone totally wrong, Rhys is stunned when the bride-to-be sets his blood on fire.

A modern pack princess...
Celina Monaghan will do anything for her father and pack—well, almost anything. The idea of an arranged marriage to a strange Wolf in this day and age has the feminist side of this Dallas Fire & Rescue EMT bent all the hell out of shape. She's agreed to meet this Reece Chatham guy face-to-face, but submitting to him? Nope, not gonna happen. She's holding out for a mythical true mating. Then the man she thinks is Reece walks in the door. He can't be her true mate!

A Blood Moon mating...
Surviving pack politics threatening to set the town on fire and a Blood Moon challenge to get their

happy ever after? What could possibly go wrong…besides BLOOD & FIRE!

Roxanne St. Claire's Barefoot Bay Kindle World

BAREFOOT BAY: DOUBLE TROUBLE (A Hard Target companion novella.)
When you owe a man for saving your life, calling in a favor isn't a big deal. Right?

Nicholas "Nick" Karras, hot-shot Air Force veteran once flew missions in the war zone. Now he flies under the radar. When Gabe Rossi calls in a favor, the last thing Nick expects is playing white knight to a young mother on the run.

With the lives of her twins on the line, who can she trust?
Peony "Peni" Comanescu is coerced into becoming the surrogate mother for a powerful man. He wants a son for his heir. A daughter is just a messy complication. When Peni discovers the depth of his evil, she runs away to save her newborn children. With a million-dollar bounty now on her head, Peni and her twins hide at Barefoot Bay, sheltered by strangers.

When a Romanian mobster arrives to claim his son, there's only one thing to do…
Determined to protect Peni and her children, Nick calls in reinforcements. With two babies caught in the crossfire, there's more than love at stake—there's Double Trouble for Nick and his friends.

ABOUT THE AUTHOR

Silver likes walking on the wild side and coffee. Okay. She loves coffee. LOTS of coffee. Warning: Her Muse, Iffy, runs with scissors and can be quite dangerous. An award-winning author, she's been a military officer's wife, mother, state appellate court marshal, airport rescue firefighter and forensic fire photographer, crime analyst, technical crime scene investigator, and writer of magic and mystery. Now retired from the "real world," she lives in Oklahoma and spends her days at the computer with two Newfoundland dogs, the cat who rules them all, and myriad characters all clamoring for attention. She writes dark urban fantasy thrillers, time travel romance, and sexy contemporary romance.

To find out more about Silver and her books, visit her **www.silverjames.com**. She loves to connect with readers on her Facebook fan page: **Silver James: For Readers**, and **@SilverJames_** on Twitter. Sign up for her newsletter at her website for announcements of new releases, subscriber-only contests, and free reads.

www.ingramcontent.com/pod-product-compliance
Lightning Source LLC
Chambersburg PA
CBHW061152170626
46809CB00003B/1060